GARDEN BOULEVARD

ANGELA AMMAN

Copyright © 2018 by Angela Amman

All rights reserved.

Print edition ISBN-13: 978-1717180629

No part of this book may be reproduced in any form or by any electronic or mechanical means, including information storage and retrieval systems, without written permission from the author, except for the use of brief quotations in a book review.

Garden Boulevard is a work of fiction. All resemblance to persons living or dead is purely coincidental.

Original cover photography by Evelyn Bertrand on Unsplash

Cover design by Bannerwing Books.

For my Dad
who always brought flowers

ACKNOWLEDGMENTS

The idea for Garden Boulevard sprouted from a photograph, but it never would have taken root without the guidance of a supportive village of people—those who realize they're part of it and those who might never know. Much gratitude to

writers near and far whose work draws me into their worlds so thoroughly, I seek the courage to create my own.

Jennie Goutet and Julie C. Gardner for their beta reading skills. You trusted my stories while making them stronger.

Megan Abbott, whose Instagram account inspires me to open my eyes to what lies around me.

Janel Mills, who polished my manuscript with a critical eye and honest commentary. I appreciate the way you called me out on writing quirks weighing down my words.

Ryan, Abbey, and Dylan, who (usually) never complain when

my mind wanders to fictional places instead of making real dinners.

Cameron Garriepy and Mandy Dawson, without whom this book may have stayed locked in drafts forever. How do you acknowledge the writing partners who believe in you enough to keep questioning, prodding, and pushing, from plot lines to character development? Thank you, my friends. I hope the echo of my gratitude finds its way to you when you most need it.

CONTENTS

MORE THAN A PECK	1
INTERLUDE	15
ON HER TERMS	19
INTERLUDE	29
LESSONS IN LIMITS	33
INTERLUDE	43
SYMBIOSIS	47
INTERLUDE	55
AT THE TERMINAL	59
INTERLUDE	69
ABOVE THE CITY	73
INTERLUDE	91
CHASING STROLLERS	97
INTERLUDE	107
THE INSTALLATION	111
Also by Angela Amman	147
Excerpt from Nothing Goes Away	149
Excerpt from Metaphysical Gravity	151
Excerpt from Joy	153
About Angela Amman	157
About the Publisher	159

GARDEN BOULEVARD

MORE THAN A PECK

BETH

"How was the beauty parlor today?" Grace Ellen asked, pulling her key out of the mailbox in the lobby. Her knobbed fingers clutched the coupon mailers and other junk so many of the residents fished out of their boxes each day.

Beth smiled. Meeting her elderly neighbor in the lobby was one of the most predictable parts of her life. Grace Ellen always seemed to be getting her mail just as Beth was coming in after work, even though Beth's schedule varied by day. Hearing the salon where she worked called a "beauty parlor" was jarring at first, but Beth grew accustomed to it, the way Grace Ellen's talcum powder soon seemed like the lobby's only scent.

"Busy," Beth said. "Spring means lots of brides, coming in for highlights, coming in to practice their wedding day hair, debating extensions." She unlocked her own mailbox without much enthusiasm. She and Grant received very little actual mail, but the few times Grace Ellen had noticed her walking upstairs without peeking into the box, she'd been aghast. *You just never know what you'll miss, honey.* With her hair perpetually set and lipstick perpetually applied, the elderly woman was intent on not missing out on anything.

"Mmm hmm," Grace Ellen said. "All these beautiful girls worrying so much about their weddings and so little about their actual marriages."

"I don't know if that's necessarily true," Beth said, voice gentle enough not to be an argument. She'd seen enough brides to know their motivation varied as much as paint shades for the color white. She wasn't, however, going to argue with a woman who had been widowed for only two years, after over sixty years of marriage. Grace Ellen had her opinions, but for the most part she was harmless.

"One thing I know is true is you're the toughest woman I know, wearing those shoes all day and probably only sitting down when you finally get home," Grace Ellen said. It was another one of the comments she recycled, even more frequently the last few months. Beth didn't like to think about what that might mean. Grace Ellen had been the first person she and Grant had met when they moved into their renovated brownstone apartment. Beth couldn't imagine what would happen when Grace Ellen could no longer live in her one-bedroom apartment on her own.

Besides, her feet did ache by the time she got home each night, no matter how thick of a platform she wore on her heels. In fact, she wasn't sure she could wear them for a moment longer. Leaning against the plate glass facing the street, she pulled off each shoe with a sigh. Grace Ellen's eyes followed her, lighting on something outside the glass.

"Now what do you suppose happened there?" Grace Ellen's words held the promise of a mystery, and Beth looked outside.

What she really wanted to do was walk upstairs and pour a glass of wine, but when an eighty-seven-year-old sounded excited about something, it made sense to listen for just a few more minutes. The only thing that looked even slightly out of the ordinary was a dirty floral bouquet resting in the middle of the sidewalk. Beth smiled at her neighbor, though she didn't find the flowers quite as interesting as Grace Ellen did. She'd likely stepped over them on her way into the building without thinking twice about it.

"I guess it's a little strange that someone left their flowers on the ground," Beth said. Strange if you didn't get out much, maybe, but the streets of the city offered countless surprises each time she walked from her home to the salon where she worked, only blocks away.

"No, honey, that's not what I meant. Just look. All them flowers are scattered around the ground. Each of the stems is absolutely bare."

Beth nodded absently, her mind already halfway up the stairs. Disappointed by Beth's waning interest, Grace Ellen sighed.

"Let me walk on up with you, hon. I got something for you. Had something delivered really. I don't get out as much as I used to."

Feeling chastised, though she wasn't sure why, Beth leaned over and linked her arm through Grace Ellen's.

"I can't wait to see," she said.

"It's more you can't wait to *taste*," Grace Ellen said, pleased with her own little surprise.

~

Beth leaned against the washing machine as it churned to life, beginning her least favorite part of her Saturday night routine. She used to wash their sheets after work on Mondays and Fridays, knowing how much Grant hated to see evidence of laundry and how much he loved the scent of lavender on his pillowcases. Early in their marriage, she timed things impeccably with her work schedule and she relished that, one of the little puzzle pieces that made their relationship magic and private and immune to piles of laundry on Saturday mornings.

Grant used to bring her coffee in bed on Saturdays, though he'd had to wake before sunrise to beat her alarm. On Friday nights, their bed became a lavender-scented oasis against responsibilities, but Saturday mornings brought overscheduled days at the salon. What he did during the day stayed shrouded in brief answers about golf games with people she didn't know, but every Saturday she woke to fresh coffee, and he'd be waiting for her with takeout from their favorite sushi place when she got home. Those days felt like another life.

She didn't have to time the wash cycle any longer.

Lately, she could wait until she got home from the salon any day of the week before tossing in the armful of Egyptian cotton sheets. They would still be dried and stretched over the king-sized mattress long before he walked in the door. Grant's hours crept upward with his promotions, as had something bordering on arrogance. She never let herself say the word aloud, just as she didn't allow herself to linger on the way he glossed over her news about clients, glossed over her conversations, glossed over her tentative questions about stopping her birth control pills.

As she closed the door on the laundry closet, she absently scrolled through her phone. Not surprisingly, nothing much had changed since she'd checked earlier in the day. Her social calendar had cleared significantly since Grant's latest promotion. His vitriol at her once-frequent girls' nights had grown when he had to back away from his weekly poker night. Now their evenings were often spent talking around current events neither of them particularly cared about, just to fill the silence in the home.

Every few months, laughter crept back into his eyes. Less stress at work, maybe something in the air, Beth could never predict when the old Grant would emerge. He would, though, just when she felt the most alone. On those nights, he'd take her out somewhere she couldn't begin to know how to get reservations to, though she knew enough never to mention how much she missed the dive bars they would find during their dating years.

A brusque text popped onto her screen, letting her know he was ordering dinner in to the office. Exhausted by the idea of cooking and cleaning for herself for the third time this week, she poured cereal and Chardonnay into lonely kitchenware, grabbing her book and tucking her legs under a chenille throw on the couch. The book occupied the spaces in her brain not automatically calculating the time between washing and drying and smoothing warm sheets over her bed.

He sniffed the kitchen when he meandered home well after nightfall, and she might have called his expression a sneer if she would have raised her eyes from her Chardonnay to meet his glance. Instead she swirled the wine, watching the feet trace down the glass, not caring at all about any of the things she'd learned in her wine appreciation event at their new country club.

"Why does it smell like peaches in here?"

"Grace Ellen bought us a little bag of them," Beth said, biting back a sigh. "I think it's called a peck."

"Who the hell is Grace Ellen?" he asked, his eyes skittering around the countertop for the offending fruit. "Why didn't you tell her we don't eat peaches?"

Agitated, he pulled at his tie. Expensive swirls of paisley drooped from his collar and pulled his mouth down into a petulant frown, and she couldn't even muster the energy to be impressed by the way the emerald pattern pulled out the hint of green in his eyes.

"You know Grace Ellen, Grant. She lives right across...." Her words lifted into the air above his head. She could have been saying anything at all.

"I mean, we hate peaches," he said, his words trailing behind him as he strode into the living room, away from the offending smell.

His irritated stomps paused long enough for him to grab his glass of whiskey from the bar cart before retreating into the small den, letting the thump of his briefcase against the polished wood floor punctuate his displeasure. She could hear the rattling of the whiskey stones against the heavy crystal she'd inherited from her grandmother before it was covered by the sounds of the Yankees game on his expensive TV. She knew she'd clear the glass out of the den later, carefully washing the crystal by hand and drying it to stash it out of sight. Grant couldn't stand to see things drying on the counters, and she didn't have the energy to break the habits she'd formed before she realized her husband's predilections didn't have to be hers.

"No. You. You hate peaches," she whispered.

She hefted the ripening fruit from the kitchen table, where it was couched in shadows. Dumping the peaches into the garbage can in the kitchen wouldn't be enough; Grant would smell them, and his comments would escalate quickly from petulant to cruel. The garbage chute in the hallway was a better choice, and by Monday they would be sitting on the curb and waiting to be dumped into the belly of the rumbling waste management truck.

Beth couldn't remember the last time she'd eaten a peach. Her grocery list remained the same each week, and she struck peaches from it long before she and Grant had gotten married. Visiting his business school friends in Georgia one summer, he'd gone on a rant about the offending fruit. His old roommates could barely breathe by the end of the tirade. She'd laughed, too, come to think of it, still thinking his opinions stemmed from passion and not inflexibility.

She quickly walked to the garbage chute with the fruit in her arms, trying to remember the way the sweet flesh would feel against her tongue. The soft fuzz of the peach flesh rolled against her fingers, and Beth paused before opening the door to dispose of the fruit. Tossing something Grace Ellen had been so pleased to offer made tears prick at Beth's eyelids. Before she could talk herself out of it, she abruptly returned to their apartment, the bag of peaches clutched against her chest.

It wouldn't hurt to keep the fruit in her minuscule pantry cupboard for a single night.

∽

Beth woke before dawn on Sunday morning, tying running shoes and closing the door quietly so as not to wake her husband. Sundays were a dance for them, perfectly timed so he would be on his way to the office just minutes before she came back through the lobby. Brunches and lazy Sundays were wisps of memories, replaced by the rigid structure that let them slide close to each other but not close enough to touch before moving forward with their days.

Blood pounded in her ears as she circled back home. On Sundays she ran without music, the weight of her thoughts the closest thing she had to a confessional. Cool morning light replaced the pre-dawn streetlights, and she used the steps outside her building to stretch her tired legs. Remembering Grace Ellen's piqued curiosity, she looked at the ground, but nothing remained of the detached roses. Though she hadn't cared much about them the day before, their absence felt like a loss. Someone had purchased the roses, most likely from the newspaper stand only a few steps down the block, and now they'd been swept away with the rest of the trash that multiplied on the streets each day.

She managed to scrub both bathrooms to a sheen, shower, and finish her first cup of coffee before admitting what Grant had noticed the moment he walked into their apartment: the peaches were filling the room with their scent. She had to do something about them before he got home.

A tentative knock at the door saved her from making a decision.

Grace Ellen stood in the hallway, eyes sparkling.

"Is everything OK?" Beth asked. She regretted her tone immediately, but she didn't respond well to breaks in her carefully orchestrated routine. Grace Ellen, despite meeting her near the lobby mailboxes four days a week, rarely took the few steps across the carpet from her apartment to Beth and Grant's.

"Of course, honey. I just wanted to stop by and see if you tried any of them peaches yet?"

Beth shook her head, looking at the thin outline of Grace Ellen's lips instead of her eyes. Today's lipstick was a pale coral, and the early hour meant it hadn't yet feathered into the lines punctuating her mouth.

"You better eat 'em up fast," Grace Ellen advised. "They go bad pretty quick once they're ripe. And there's something real special about eating spring fruit that isn't even in season up here yet."

Beth nodded and blushed, though it was impossible for her neighbor to know she had almost discarded all the ripening fruit into their building's incinerator. Guilt prompted her next words. "Would you like to come in for a cup of coffee? Grant's working today." Her words were an apology, though she didn't know why.

"Oh, he is?" The question came too quickly, and Beth had to admit it was likely Grant's hours were just as familiar to their neighbor as her own seemed to be. "Thank you for the offer but I'm expecting a call from my great-grandbabies today. Plus, I haven't read my news yet. My granddaughter fixed it up so my computer goes right to my news when I turn it on. Isn't that something?"

Beth smiled, waiting until Grace Ellen's door closed before closing her own, as though the woman was walking miles home instead of just steps across the hallway. Her neighbor had never mentioned a computer before, and something about the idea flipped happily in Beth's gut. Maybe Grace Ellen wasn't quite as lonely as she seemed.

Unexpectedly bolstered, Beth pulled the peaches out of the pantry and cradled one in her hands under cool running water. With a paring knife in hand, she pulled a small china plate out of a small, rarely used cupboard at the corner of the kitchen. She had acquiesced to Grant's suggestion to put their china in the storage unit when they moved into the brownstone, but she'd tucked away a few beloved pieces. The kitchen was only a smidge larger than the postage stamp-sized one they'd left behind. It faced east, though, and the early morning light expanded the space where she reverently placed the plate and fruit on the rustic table.

She pushed the tip of the knife into the soft flesh of the peach. The blade sliced away a small section of the fruit. Acutely aware of the juice wetting her fingers, Beth brought the peach to her mouth, letting her tongue register the texture change between the fuzzy skin and succulent flesh. Her eyes closed in response.

She'd forgotten the taste, the juicy sweetness, the yielding flesh.

She didn't want to forget again.

As she swallowed, cut another slice, and swallowed again an idea blossomed. Pushing her chair away from the table, she abandoned the half-eaten fruit and strode to the counter where she clinically washed the rest of the peaches and dissected the fruit from their pits. Only when the slices rested in an oversize bowl did she wipe her hands absently on a dishtowel and begin to scroll through recipes online. Cursing when she realized she had no idea how to craft a serviceable piecrust, she clicked and scrolled until she found a recipe for peach crumble that didn't require her to wander the city for a rolling pin.

It took her longer to clean the remnants of the simple recipe from her countertops than it did to put it together, and she was reading on the couch again when the first aroma began drifting through the apartment.

∽

Years of teaching herself restraint came in handy as she waited for the crumble to finish baking. For the last ten minutes, she didn't turn off the oven light, willing the textured top to begin to brown and crisp. When she could hardly wait any longer, she watched the clock for a solid minute before carefully removing the glass baking dish from the oven. Letting it cool seemed impossible, but she told herself there was no hurry. Grant's arrival from the office no longer pulled her to erase all vestiges of herself from her day.

Too impatient to open her book again, Beth picked up her phone, yearning to reach out to one of her friends. After tapping a few keys, she paused. Her giddiness felt ridiculous. Jojo, her closest friend from the salon, would likely be rolling out of bed around noon on a Sunday—and she definitely wouldn't understand the significance of baking a dish Beth's husband was sure to hate. Her shoulders slumped. How had she gotten to a place where she didn't even have a girlfriend to call on a Sunday morning?

Fighting the urge to carry the baking dish into the hall with her and toss the whole thing down the chute, Beth pulled back her shoulders and opened the front door. Five steps and thirty seconds later, and she was facing Grace Ellen for the second time that day.

"Well, hi there," Grace Ellen said, and Beth forced herself to ignore the surprise in her neighbor's voice. It had been tough enough to admit to herself that her almost ninety-year-old neighbor might be the closest thing she had to a friend.

"I was wondering if your great-grandchildren had called yet," Beth said. "I…well…I made a little crumble with those peaches, and I wondered if you wanted to try some with a cup of tea?"

Grace Ellen beamed. "Well, I'd love that, I think. They did call. Right after church is when we like to chat. Not that I go on over to the church every Sunday anymore, but that's still when they like to call."

Grace Ellen pulled her keys off a little hook on the side of the door and locked it behind her.

"Now, you don't mind if I just wear my house shoes on over, do you? I suppose I could put on something a little nicer, but it's not as if we're going for a walk outside."

Beth looked down at her own mismatched running socks and tamped down a smile.

"Of course not. I want you to be comfortable."

Mentally crossing her fingers that she hadn't botched the recipe too badly, Beth scooped some of the crumble for both of them, using her china for the second time that day. Grace Ellen had already made herself comfortable at the kitchen table, neatly pushing the half-eaten peach that remained there to the center of the table. Steam wafted from the pieces, and Grace Ellen beamed at the plate Beth placed in front of her.

"What a beautiful china pattern! Mine has poppies. I've always loved those flowers, and I even insisted on naming our oldest Penelope just so I could call her Poppy. My Alfred didn't mind. He was just overwhelmed by the idea of living with two females. All brothers in his house, you see."

Beth nodded. She hadn't known, of course, that Alfred had had only brothers or even that Poppy was named for her mother's favorite flower.

"You wouldn't happen to have any vanilla ice cream, would you?" Grace Ellen's eyes sparkled as though the women were doing something illicit by having dessert just past noon.

"I do," Beth said, pulling the pint from the freezer and deftly scooping some onto Grace Ellen's crumble. She hesitated before leaving her own naked. She only wanted to taste the flavor of the peaches.

Grace Ellen took a bite and murmured appreciatively before carefully placing her fork across the side of her plate.

"I'm surprised, you know. That you made this. You seemed a little put out when I passed along the peck of peaches."

Regret ballooned in Beth's chest.

"Oh, not at all! It's just, well, Grant isn't much of a fan of peaches."

Grace Ellen's brow furrowed for a moment before she took another bite, leveling her gaze at Beth. "My Alfred, rest his soul, was crazy for peaches. He hated my strawberry rhubarb pie, though. Just hated it. Of course, he'd laugh and laugh when the girls and I would make it. 'Are you saying I need to start watching my waistline, Gracie?' He teased me something awful. I guess your Grant isn't much of the teasing kind."

Beth forced herself to meet the caring gaze, though she felt her cheeks redden with the unspoken betrayal. "No. He's not really a teasing sort of man."

"I suppose it's hard to be beholden to a man who doesn't make you laugh," Grace Ellen said. Beth began to protest but stopped herself before defending Grant.

"I'm not sure why I feel so beholden, though," she whispered. The words, once escaped, grew into something real.

Grace Ellen nodded.

"I keep telling you, honey. You're the toughest woman I know. Maybe you're not as…beholden…as I was thinking you were."

Beth scraped her fork delicately along the plate, savoring the remaining bits of brown sugar and flour mixed with cinnamon-flavored peaches. There was no longer any thought of dumping out the remainder of the crumble. Perhaps Grace Ellen was right and she was, indeed, tough enough to stand on three-inch heels to look Grant in the eye and deliver an ultimatum about a baby. Maybe she was tough enough to balance on those same heels if she had to turn away from him and walk out of the home she'd quietly shaped to his wishes for the entirety of their short marriage.

Her tongue teased crumbs from the tines of the fork before she asked Grace Ellen a question about her great-grandchildren. She had waited for the crumble to bake, and now she would wait to see Grant's reaction when he met her unsheathed words.

∼

INTERLUDE

WORKING OVERTIME

My phone is in my hand, but somehow I know it's him before I glance down to see his name. I don't need to answer the phone to know what my husband needs. The only time he calls twenty minutes before he's due home to relieve the nanny is when there's no way he'll make it back to our brownstone before bedtime. Throwing my phone isn't an option. Instead of whisper-yelling my irritation practically in the cab driver's ear, I tap out a message letting him know I'll take care of it.

I can't miss the soft opening of the boutique in SoHo, so I put in a forced cheerful call to Brooke—named after the city well before she moved there—and cajole her into staying for a few more hours. The good-natured pleading, like many of my interactions lately, is only a facade. She's never said no to extra time. Brooke's on her way to paying off her grad school loans before I do, with the amount of overtime we've paid her so far this year. Her boyfriend moved back to Philly right after Valentines's Day, and she's more than willing to hang out with the kids for extra cash, and maybe even more willing to enjoy a glass of expensive wine with me when I get home.

Bobby's return text is apologetic in that way text messages can be, as long as I don't count on him actually making any changes the next time one of his meetings runs over or one of his clients wants to play the back nine for the second time. He hates that I still call him Bobby. The childhood nickname is lodged in my head now, and I can't get rid of it, the way he's lodged in my heart, even though some days I can't remember why we're even together. Quick stabs at the phone: *schedule date night*. Part of me sighs as I type, but our therapist insists this is when we really need to make the time to connect.

The cab idles. Our light is green, but there's no way the cars in front of us are budging anytime in the next thirty seconds. I glance at my watch. Traffic is the worst at this time of day, though I think that way no matter when I sink into a cab going across town. Arriving early slipped out of my control a few blocks ago, but I might manage to pull off on time. My phone pings another message. My assistant somehow materialized at the boutique before me, though I swear she'd been in the office when I left. I can hear her precision perkiness in her text: *Got here early. Everything's perfect. I don't know how you do it.*

My head aches, so I shake a few aspirin into my palm. Swallowing dry doesn't bother me anymore; I can ignore the bitterness lingering at the back of my throat. I like to pretend the medicine works more quickly this way. Wishful thinking, I'm sure, but sometimes believing in something matters.

The cab inches forward and stops again. I can close my eyes for the rest of the ride. Leaning my head against the window, I spot rose petals scattered along the ground. I'm too exhausted to wonder why they've been separated from their buds. My almost-closed eyes snap open, my fingers already swiping to add another reminder: *pick up flowers for Gigi's opening night of the school play.*

I should send the reminder to Bobby. She smiles wider when her flowers come from him, but he'd forgotten last year. We'd had to pay for the atrocities for sale in the lobby, glitter obscuring any sense of freshness from the wilting blooms. Somehow I'll make sure he has them in his arms when he sees her. He can have the credit; I just need to put it out of my head and close my eyes for fifteen minutes.

Abruptly the cab surges forward, twisting through traffic, and ending any chance at rest. Instead of leaning against the window, I use the reflection to slide burgundy gloss over my lips. The fading light masks the shadows under my eyes, but I feel them there, eyelids offering only slight relief from the grittiness caused by late nights and three too many cups of black coffee. One more reminder—*buy concealer*—and a quick squirt of eye drops before I swipe my card and leave the cab.

Three more hours, and I'll be able to kiss the kids goodnight. The thought of their sleep-heavy eyes smiling through the dark makes me smile. I wonder for a moment why it hurts my cheeks before remembering: I haven't smiled, not really, all day.

∼

ON HER TERMS

ALICIA

Alicia unlocked her door automatically, no longer thinking of the variety of locks she and Claudia employed to keep people out of their little haven in the middle of the city. Each day, before she reentered their apartment, she shook off the day: a literal toss of her head and deep breath to expel everything she didn't want creeping into her home life. A yoga teacher had mentioned doing it once, and though the woman was now somewhere in Palm Springs, calling herself a life coach and bilking retirees out of their generous investments, Alicia still liked clearing her mind before coming home.

Mail got dropped into a beautifully carved wooden box, though there were months when neither roommate went through the papers until they began to peek over the side. Nothing of importance came through the mail, anyway, and if they received anything remotely interesting, they tore into it immediately. A thick ivory envelope looked promising. She combed her thoughts for any upcoming weddings, but the only one she could think of wouldn't end up as an invitation in her box. The card turned out to be a mass mailing for a special event at a boutique called Raindrops on Roses, apparently one with a larger marketing budget than most shops in the neighborhood.

Before walking any farther, she pried off her heeled booties and bent from the waist to stretch out the backs of her legs. No one would notice if she started wearing flats to work, she knew, and no one would blame her if she did. Her friends had been shocked to learn how frequently she was on her feet at work when they'd done one of those step challenges one week. Apparently, they thought librarians sat behind desks, cleaning their glasses and waiting to answer obscure questions. Shoes made her smile, though, and the idea of giving up even an inch of her height made her cringe.

"I thought I heard you." Claudia walked out of her room, a carton of something frozen in her hand. "Are you doing yoga in the foyer?"

"No, just loosening up a little bit," Alicia said.

Claudia shuddered. "Such a waste of time, yoga."

Alicia shook her head. She and Claudia had met at the coffee shop where they both worked, Claudia while she figured out how to make songwriting work and Alicia while she figured out how to make herself work. When Claudia's great aunt decided to move to Arizona permanently, they finagled the apartment with promises not to paint the sky blue ceilings. The location was worth the blue paint, they agreed, and they managed to turn their polar differences into a comfortable living situation. Claudia had left the coffee shop to shuffle papers at a record label, but they continued to share the space under Aunt Claudia's indoor sky.

"What are you even eating?" Alicia asked. Claudia had given up dairy weeks ago, which meant she was now eschewing wheat, red meat, poultry, cruciferous vegetables, dairy, and sugar.

"Ice and air, love. Ice and air," she said, twisting the carton so Alicia could read the ingredient list of the coconut ice cream.

"Looks delicious."

"Speaking of looking delicious, your cheating hunk of a boyfriend is taking his engagement public tomorrow night." Claudia spooned another bite of the faux ice cream into her mouth. "I used to wish you were the one he planned on marrying, but I really think you ended up with the better end of the whole deal."

Alicia expected to be shocked but felt mostly indifferent about the announcement. "I don't think I have either end of any sort of deal, to be honest. And if you mean he's having an engagement party, I'm not surprised. What a perfect photo op for a future politician."

"Is that what he is?" Claudia asked. "I can't keep track of what he's doing with his trust fund this week."

"The engagement is already public, anyway," Alicia said. "They became public property the moment she walked into the open air with that ring."

∼

She and Julia had come face to face after a spin class, both covered in a sheen of sweat that somewhat leveled the playing field between them. Until that moment, Alicia had believed her presence was unfelt in Julia's life, though the woman with a halo of strawberry blonde curls was a specter in her own. Alicia had tried the spin studio on a whim, and she stayed when she noticed Julia took classes there regularly. She pretended that wasn't the reason why, but she'd never been all that interested in spinning until then.

Finally seeing Julia up close, Alicia hated how she appeared to be glowing instead of sweating, as if she hadn't just finished a killer fitness class. She'd hoped Julia would be less attractive than she appeared in photos, but Julia was actually more so, exuding an ethereal quality that didn't translate through a photographer's lens. Jefferson never spoke of her, but he had never denied her existence or promised Alicia he would stop seeing her.

"I know," Julia said, "where you fit into Jefferson's life."

The remark should have rankled Alicia, should have drawn out her most steely glare. Claudia had doubled over in laughter when she learned what Alicia did during the day. *"A librarian?"* she asked. *"I would have guessed assassin with your attitude."* The words shoved Alicia into a compartment in someone else's story, reduced her to something to be dealt with rather than someone with a legitimate relationship. Julia's voice, though, made it hard to feel anything but confusion. Resigned and wise, it almost sounded regal.

"I don't know what to say to that," Alicia said, searching for the right words.

"You don't have to say anything," Julia said. Alicia noted Julia's hands were folded together, her water bottle tucked under her arm. None of it made sense to her, not the words and not why Julia wouldn't have her massive engagement ring on display. Alicia and Claudia had pored over the close-up online when a gossip site published a photo. They did shots of tequila first, choking back alcohol while both of them pretended they weren't jealous of the family sapphire now sitting on the slim finger of an ex-ballerina.

"He loves me," Alicia blurted, cringing at the words as soon as they left her lips. She wasn't completely sure it was true. And it didn't matter. Not really. It hadn't since she'd seen the article about the engagement, since she had left it front and center on her coffee table. He hadn't even had the decency to turn it over. He laughed and used it as a coaster, and she pretended to be indifferent to all of it.

"That's immaterial," Julia said.

Alicia wanted to claw out the calm eyes staring at her, though she had never considered resorting to physical violence in her life. The desire came from the utter calm exuding from the woman in front of her. This moment had played out in Alicia's mind, daydreams involving confrontational tears, though she was never quite sure which of them would be crying.

"We'll see," Alicia said, unsure of what else to say.

"I think you're misunderstanding me," Julia said, her voice puzzled. "I'm not asking you to give him up. I'm not telling you to stay away from him. I just wanted to acknowledge it. As soon as I learned who you were, it bothered me that you might think I didn't know."

Silence ballooned. Alicia felt herself swallowing compulsively, but there wasn't anything to say.

Julia spoke instead. "I guess I'm just saying you can have him."

She thought, for a couple of confusing weeks, that the conversation had meant Julia was planning to leave Jefferson. She expected an uptick in phone calls, weeknight dates, maybe a change in his mood. But everything had remained the same until Claudia texted her the link to the engagement announcement.

She never saw Julia at the spin studio again.

The encounter felt like a secret between them, and in the days that followed it would become one. Alicia had wanted to throw it in Jeff's face a million times since then, but something about the resignation in Julia's voice led Alicia to understand she didn't have a clue what kept Jefferson and Julia together. Each day that passed, each day she didn't mention it to him or to Claudia, it seemed less and less real. Julia did a wedding photo shoot in a local publication shortly after the engagement announcement spread over social media, one that carefully noted that the dresses she'd been photographed in were simply props. The illusion only added to the otherworldliness of the engagement. Emotion never seemed to mar her expression, and Alicia tried to figure out which of the dresses reflected her personality, which of the floral arrangements. She wondered why the beatific smile never reached those calm eyes.

∽

"You can do a million times better than him," Claudia said.

"You're right. Attractive men with family money are so easy to find." Alicia meant her words to be sarcastic, but Claudia laughed.

"Actually, if that's what you're looking for, your chances are probably better in Manhattan than most places," she said, shrugging. Claudia's boyfriend didn't have an iota of family money, but he was hilarious and loyal and mostly charming, except for the couple of months when he'd decided to stop sleeping in solid chunks after hearing that Einstein slept in blocks and took naps during the day.

"You're probably right," Alicia said. She hadn't known she was looking for someone with money until she met Jefferson. Even now, the shine on it had faded.

"I'm jumping in the shower, and then I think we need to get out of here and find some fun," Claudia said. She spun on her heel before Alicia could argue.

The knock at the door didn't startle her, though he usually called before coming over. His unaffected interest had slid into eagerness, which she found tiring, especially with the recent developments in his other relationship. She wondered why he hadn't buzzed, who had let him into the building. She hoped it hadn't been Grace Ellen. Her elderly neighbor seemed to know there was something not exactly right about her relationship. A few times she'd tried to engage Alicia in conversation about it, conversations that started with fairly innocent questions and ended with Alicia getting cooler and more distant with each answer.

∼

"We need to talk," he said, striding through her door like he did through every door. She'd never seen him hesitate before entering a room, never seen him take a breath to assess if he had a right to be where he was. Even after his engagement had been splashed all over social media, they kept trying new restaurants, walking hand-in-hand through crowded dining rooms. They were photographed a couple of times, but Jefferson had the money to make sure those images disappeared before they became public. Alicia wondered if Julia realized he made deals with paparazzi to share just enough of their lives to keep people interested.

"Claudia's here," Alicia said. His posture meant he actually had something to say.

He shrugged. He had never found her roommate particularly interesting.

"I'm sure you're aware of what's taking place tomorrow evening," he said.

She was. She shook her head in the negative anyway.

He ran his hand through his hair, though she noticed him glance quickly at the mirror in the hall to make sure he hadn't done egregious style damage.

"Let's sit down. I thought you were aware the engagement party was taking place tomorrow," Jefferson said. Alicia noted with vague interest that he didn't claim ownership of it, though she would have bet his family was footing the bill, that he'd chosen each of the menu items himself.

"I must have misplaced my invitation," Alicia said, cooling her voice as much as she could.

"Don't be absurd. I want to talk with you about it, because it's happening very near here."

That was information she hadn't known, and it stung. He was beginning to annoy her, but it rankled to know he would be toasting his bride-to-be anywhere in the vicinity of her carved-out city niche. Her face remained still, but her mind raced, trying to figure out where a society-friendly event would take place in her neighborhood. Coffee shops, art galleries the size of a postcard, dive bars and a few new restaurants mingled with boutiques, but nothing highbrow came to mind. He held her hands in his, stroking her skin. She let him, because it was easier than pulling away.

"Interesting," she said. "I'll make sure to remain inside so as not to embarrass you with my scarlet letter."

"Don't." His lips turned down instead of up. Sarcasm didn't work on him. He never pretended to be anything he wasn't, and he bristled equally at her subtle digs and attempts at humor.

She sat on the couch, impassive, flexing her sore feet. She never thought to offer him something to drink, though she couldn't recall another visit where she hadn't catered to him the moment he walked through the door.

"It's at the Whitney Building," he said.

Blood drained from her face. She could feel coolness in her cheeks, and then heat as it flooded back, making the room spin. She wrenched her hands from his.

"The Whitney Building?" she repeated. "Isn't that a private residence?"

He nodded. "About 20 units."

Her nails bit into her palms as she tried to ground her thoughts, to concentrate on what he was saying.

"Julia moved into the top floor unit a few weeks ago. I'll be living there after the wedding."

The spinning stopped, and she uncurled her fingers from her hands.

"You can leave now." She should have said those words to him the moment she realized he never intended to choose between her and Julia.

"I was just—"

"Just telling me that you moved your fiancée into the building next to my home? You could live anywhere in this city, or almost anywhere. I guess I don't know exactly how much money you actually have, but you're telling me you chose here? Did you think it was clever to set up your wife-to-be and your lover on the same city block?"

Her hands felt like ice, and she focused on the coldness, willing her tears to stay locked inside her chest.

"Now you're being ridiculous. I didn't choose it. I'm many things, but I'd like to think I'm not intentionally cruel."

"You should have discouraged her, then," Alicia said.

"Discouraged her? Oh, God, you think Julia chose that place? No. She couldn't care less where... Never mind how we got there. I just needed you to know it was happening."

"Now I know, and now I need you to know what's *happening*. This is finished. Done."

"Nothing is changing," Jefferson said, cupping her chin in his hand for a split second before she batted it away.

She wasn't a child.

"Everything already changed."

"Alicia. I love—"

"That's immaterial." Julia's words came back to her, and they seemed fitting. "I don't need you to love me."

"I don't even know what that's supposed to mean," he said. She hated the whining exasperation in his voice, the tone that let her know he was accustomed to getting what he wanted.

"I wouldn't expect you to," she said.

"What makes today different than any of the other days?" he asked, softening his voice.

Alicia let his voice soothe her, feeling her resolve weaken until she looked out the window of the small, rent-controlled brownstone unit and saw the towering building where he'd be living with his wife. Julia had been willing to share him, it seemed. She wasn't.

∽

INTERLUDE

VINYL LIES

*H*e left a couple of folded bills on the cheap bookcase next to the bed, with a note about taking a cab instead of the subway. I blinked at the smiley face he'd sketched under his name, and I wanted to sweep his albums onto the floor. I was charmed by his vinyl collection the first time I visited, but then he admitted he hadn't gotten around to picking up a turntable yet. It should have been a sign he wasn't the person I thought, but blue eyes and a killer vocabulary have always clouded my eyes more than logic.

My head screamed as I sat up, and I pressed my fingers against my eyes. Mascara flakes riddled my fingertips and cheeks, and I longed for a cold glass of water. I always kept one next to my bed at home. I hadn't drunk that much the night before, but apparently cheap shooters at the bar wreaked havoc on my body in a way a good glass of wine never would. I pushed flashes of the night out of my head, feeling tears threatening. I could see the remnants of last night's crying on his pillowcase, and my stomach roiled when I thought about how I just should have gone home after last call.

I stumbled a little on the way to the bathroom. An almost-hysterical laugh escaped my sore throat when I considered it a miracle that he'd already left for class or work or wherever he'd gone this morning. Warm water took care of my raccoon eyes, and I felt a savage satisfaction when my face left black stains of mascara on his pristine beige towel. I'd used his toothbrush before, after a movie marathon that left both of us too exhausted for me to return to my own place. We slept back to back in his platform bed that night, and I felt so safe drifting into slumber near him.

I wouldn't use his toothbrush today, choosing instead to shove a toothpaste-covered finger into my mouth, wiping it across my teeth before compulsively scraping my tongue the best I could with my fingernails. I had to get out of there before my stomach rebelled.

My skirt was pooled on the floor, and when I tried to close the torn zipper, I couldn't stop my tears. Grabbing everything that belonged to me, I stared at the money sitting atop the particleboard bookcase filled with useless vinyl. I reached for it, but the bills felt dirty, and I dropped them as quickly as I grabbed them. I took the note, though, crumpling it in my fist for the moment because I couldn't stand to look at his scratched letters scrawled across the paper. The smiling salutation mocked me.

I had dropped my last dollar bills onto the bar in a blur of laughter just before the bar closed. I knew better than to go out without a credit card, but I had more than one lapse in judgment the night before. I could picture my card sitting next to my laptop in our crowded apartment. My roommate and I had been buying tickets for a concert only minutes before our friends arrived to head to the bar, and I hadn't thought to pick up the slim piece of plastic. I dug in my clutch for my MetroCard, but I couldn't find that either, and

I started to wonder if I drank more than I remembered last night.

The money he left re-entered my thoughts, but I couldn't bring myself to take his cash after what happened. Again, my stomach lurched, and I blinked hard against the bits of memory threatening to add to the tears I just dried. I could walk. I had to walk. I didn't even hesitate when I grabbed my shoes from near the front door and pushed my sore toes into the heels. The towering platforms looked perfect on a Friday night, but they were telling on a Saturday morning, and I knew exactly how I looked as I began walking down the street. I pulled my silky tank down lower on my waist, though logic told me no one could see the rip in the skirt. No one could see how shattered I felt.

A block away from his apartment, shock settled into a combination of anger and pain. I thought I could pretend everything was ok, but my thighs brushed together painfully with each step. I didn't know if I would see his fingerprints bruised against my flesh when I got home, but I could feel them there, throbbing with the truth about what had happened. I waited for the light to change, my toe a stuttering staccato against the street. I couldn't look up to see who shared the corner with me, so my eyes swept my surroundings. A broken bouquet rested near the curb, and I kicked it savagely. My foot failed to make a square landing, and the stems only moved a few inches.

Tears pushed out of my eyelids again, and I should have brushed them away, but I didn't. I couldn't scream, so I would wear my anguish on my face. The light blinked for me to walk, and I stepped off the curb with a jolt, staring at the cabs lining the street and wondering how beautifully different things would have been this morning if I had climbed into one of them last night instead of wandering home with someone I thought I could trust. On the other side of the street, I uncurled my fingers from his note, ripping into it and obliterating it into jagged bits of nothing. I tossed them in the air, wishing I could ride away with them on the wind, wishing I could be anywhere and anyone but me.

∼

LESSONS IN LIMITS

SPENCER

Spencer rested her hands on top of her laptop for a full minute, trying to talk herself into working on her philosophy paper. After all, she had dragged everything she needed all the way to the library to finish the dreaded assignment. In a huff, she pushed her computer closed, crossing her fingers that inspiration would strike later in the day. Purple pens and random note cards lay strewn around the wobbly table, but looking through them again wouldn't do much. It hadn't the last three times she did it. Pulling her hair into a sloppy bun, she nudged her roommate.

"Cat," Spencer whispered.

Cat's fingers sped over her own keyboard. Cat could have finished her paper in the middle of a monsoon if necessary.

"Cat!" Spencer whispered again, more insistent. She did it with a furtive glance at the librarian. She'd been intrigued by the librarian all year. Like so many people Spencer had encountered since moving to New York, the librarian belied every stereotype Spencer had. Once, she hypothesized to Cat she was fairly sure the curvy librarian had appeared in a series of billboard ads about sexually transmitted diseases.

Cat had shrugged, uninterested in the woman sitting imperially behind the circulation desk.

"Spencer Claire. You have a paper due in the morning, and I'm pretty sure you've got a shift at the cafe tonight."

"Catherine Claire. You have a better handle on my schedule than I do," Spencer said. "Besides, I called off work earlier today. And why are we using our middle names about something as unimportant as a term paper?"

"You do know you're going to get fired," Cat said, fingers still flying. "And term papers are hardly unimportant." When she noticed Spencer's closed laptop, she sighed and saved her work.

"Maybe. I don't think so," Spencer said. Cat was probably right, but one of the beautiful parts of the city was that waitressing jobs waited on every corner—and in the cafes next to the corner cafes and the bars in between.

"Only someone from Nebraska could be so damn cheerful about being fired," Cat said.

"Only someone from Long Island would refuse to remember I'm actually from Ohio," Spencer said. She turned Cat's computer toward her, groaning when she saw the page count racked up at the bottom of the screen. "You're almost done!"

"Yes. I'm almost finished with the paper due tomorrow. The one assigned about seven years ago," Cat said. Even with everything almost in order, Spencer noticed her roommate's nails were bitten to the quick. Cat's father had her advisor on speed dial, and Spencer knew her roommate was beyond stressed about her final grades.

"Let's go get lunch," Spencer said, closing Cat's laptop.

"You're late, dear. We're closer to dinner," Cat said.

Spencer shifted her eyes to the east-facing windows, searching for a sign the afternoon was fading into evening. She hadn't actually called her boss about not coming into work tonight; she meant to do it after she finished the first draft of her paper, but it now seemed a little redundant to say she wouldn't be there when it was about ninety minutes into her shift. She breathed deeply and turned back to look at the librarian.

"So, why do you think the librarian looks like she's ready to don full latex and take on the evils of the world?" Spencer let her chin fall into her hands while she stared at the woman currently staring at a computer screen with a venomous look on her face.

"Spencer. Enough with the librarian theories, ok?" Cat said.

"Don't you wonder about people?" Spencer didn't know why she asked. She and Cat had had similar conversations almost since the day they'd collided in the minuscule dorm room they shared.

"I wonder about you," Cat said. It was about the closest Cat came to teasing, and Spencer decided to accept it.

"Let's go get dinner," Spencer said, gathering her things into her sagging canvas bag. Cat sighed, checking the time on her phone.

"Fine. But no parties until our papers are finished."

"That's kind of unfair," Spencer said. "Yours is going to be done in about eleven minutes, and I probably have to take an incomplete on mine."

Cat looked concerned, and Spencer wished she had kept the tone light. "Spence…."

"Let's get a drink with our dinner," Spencer said. "It will help me feel a little better about the incomplete."

"The only place we can get a drink with dinner happens to be next door to the cafe you're supposed to be working at tonight," Cat reminded her.

Spencer shrugged. Cat was right, of course. Cat had been right about ninety-five percent of the time since Spencer met her, which Spencer found both fascinating and infuriating. She also considered the anxious, willowy brunette the closest thing she had to a best friend, despite the flurry of texts she shuffled through each day.

"We could eat at the dorm and do shots of cheap liquor in our room," she said.

Cat wrinkled her nose, like it wasn't what they'd done countless times during their freshman year. "Or we could stay here and get everything finished before going home."

"Come home…." Spencer said. Her voice trailed upwards, and she tried to fill it with the promise of something fun. Cat wasn't always persuaded by fun, but the stress of finals might tip things her way. Spencer paused, watching her friend's shoulders for a sign of capitulation. She knew Cat's answer a heartbeat before Cat began gathering her computer and impeccably organized notes into her leather tote. Spencer didn't even want to think about how much the tote cost; she liked thinking she and her roommate were starting on a level playing field.

They were walking out of the library when Spencer looked back at the librarian once more. "I would love to know her story," she said.

"I don't know, Spence. I don't think it's anywhere close to as glamorous as you might imagine," Cat said.

"Why do you say that?" Spencer asked. "Did you see those biceps?"

"What I saw were bloodshot eyes and chewed up fingernails. And I know about chewed up fingernails," Cat said.

"See?" Spencer wasn't about to be distracted. "I knew you were interested!"

"You're ridiculous," Cat said. "Did you know librarians used to live in the libraries here? In apartments above the main library areas?"

Spencer stopped walking, swiveling on one heel to face a

surprised Cat. Her eyes shone with wonder, letting Cat see what Spencer must have looked like as a ten-year-old. "You've got to be kidding me! Your brain's a vault of mysterious secrets."

Cat sighed. "I wasn't trying to keep anything from you. I just never thought about it until right now."

Spencer's mind sped through a million scenarios. "Do you think your parents would want to buy us one of those apartments and renovate it for us?"

Cat's laughter, when it wasn't filled with cynicism, made Spencer smile. Musical and throaty, it made her seem like a Prohibition-era heiress. The truth was close, but it wasn't nearly as romantic. "Oh, Spencer. You're like this adorable puppy who doesn't understand that the dog park is actually just a giant fenced-in yard."

"I'd be insulted by that if I hadn't been called so much worse by half the people in my life," Spencer said. "I guess that means we're not moving out of the dorms next year."

"We might be moving out of the dorms, but it will be into a postage stamp-sized studio where you're going to have to get used to Jackson's smelly socks."

Spencer smiled. "I don't even know if NYU is going to want me anywhere near their campus next year, so your boyfriend's socks are currently the least of my concerns."

Cat's brow furrowed just as quickly as her laughter had filled the stairwell. "Don't say that. Spencer, you don't want to end up back in Ohio."

"I'm not going back to Ohio. No matter what. I was talking to that sound guy Jackson brought over the other night, and he was mentioning some theater production, and…."

"Spencer. Even the people who want to be actresses don't always figure out how to make it as actresses here," Cat said.

"Oh, I know," Spencer said. Cat's anxiety crashed against

her optimism and fell to the ground.

∼

"We should have just studied here," Spencer said, switching her tote bag to the other shoulder as they walked into their building.

"You would have gotten even less done," Cat said.

Spencer shrugged. "Maybe. Maybe not. I didn't get much done there, to be honest."

Cat sighed and then smiled. "It looks like someone's waiting for you."

Spencer's heart sped up when she saw the shape of the slumped shoulders sitting on the floor outside their door, furiously texting or drafting something on his oversized phone. She'd hoped she would talk to him today. She wished, just for a moment, that Cat wouldn't have been with her. Certain things were tough to explain. Cat stopped for a minute when they reached the door, and she shot a confused glance at Spencer before unlocking the door and disappearing inside.

"Hi!" Spencer said.

Richard scrambled to his feet, but he wouldn't meet her eyes, and her easy kiss missed its mark as he turned his head.

"I have to talk to you," he said.

"I know," Spencer said. "Want to come inside?"

"Spencer, no. We can't talk about this where your roommate can hear," he said. He steered her back down the hall, and they sank onto the steps on the side of the building.

"There's no way I'm going to finish this paper on time, Richard. I've been at the cafe so much, and I just haven't had time to really get my research together, and…."

He took off his glasses—she loved the way the tortoiseshell looked with the warm amber of his eyes—and pressed his fingers into his sockets, rubbing at them like his head hurt. "Working. Parties. Getting lost in the Met. I know what you've been doing," he said.

She frowned at the strain she heard there. "You told me it wasn't a huge deal if I turned in my paper late. You said you could fudge the date a little with Professor—"

"It's not just the paper, Spence."

"What do you mean?" Spencer asked, eyes widening. She hadn't meant to date the teaching assistant for her philosophy class, but as she struggled to keep up with the reading and the coursework, she found it offered a little safety net.

"I was going over your scores on everything else, and I just don't see how you're going to pass this class."

"That's impossible!" Spencer said. "You told me I was doing ok, that you could help me make up some of what I'd missed."

"I know what I said." His voice was agitated, and she felt a weight on her chest.

"You can't help me or you won't help me?" she asked.

"It's not that I don't want you to pass this class. I do. But…."

"I'm not asking you to change my grades, Richard," she said, feeling defensive and a little confused.

"Well, thank goodness, because I definitely wouldn't be able to do that for you. I mean, we barely know each other, not really. And I'm counting on working with Gene on my dissertation," he said. He probably would have said more, but Spencer wasn't going to let him see her cry.

"Then I better get back inside and finish this paper," she said, forcing cheer into her words.

"Spencer. I don't think you understand. I just don't think you can possibly pass this course. You're going to have to retake it."

Blinking, she thought of the conditions of her small

scholarship, trying to remember what it said about failing classes. Either way, more classes meant more debt and more hours working and more phone calls home where she pretended she had everything under control. Which she would, she promised herself; she could pull it together during summer classes.

She cupped his face in her hands, feeling so much older than Richard. His parents paid his bills every semester, at least that's what she'd sussed out when he started talking about taking low-paying research jobs for additional experience instead of tending bar like his roommate. She softened her eyes, letting him off the hook, and pressed a quick kiss against his lips. She wouldn't answer his calls again, not for a while, but he didn't have to know that now.

Spencer fell into her room, surprised to feel her chest heaving with sobs. She hadn't meant to cry this hard when she closed the door. She could tell Cat had been waiting in anticipation since she left her friend in the hallway with the man she recognized as their teacher.

"You could have talked to me about it, Spence," Cat said.

Spencer smiled, shocked that her eyes were so swollen with tears that it hurt for her cheeks to press into the top of her face.

"Probably," Spencer said. "But exactly how do I talk to you about it, when you've got everything together, and I'm basically counting on a teaching assistant to keep my ass in school?"

"Well, first of all, I would have told you to kick his balls all the way back to Brooklyn. You're much too smart to be depending on him for anything," Cat said.

"Cat. Don't be crazy. I can't even remember the last time I

went to my chem class."

"Well, there's your mistake, then," Cat said. "You should have tried dating your chem teaching assistant. You could write your way out of your philosophy class with your eyes closed."

"Too early for your ridiculous jokes," Spencer said, but her tears already felt less urgent. She glanced in the mirror, wiping mascara from under her eyes with her pinky fingers. Her manicure was a mess. Thankfully, she had a little bit of money leftover this week, and she could probably skip a few lunches and eke out a mani—if she still had a job in the morning.

"Honey. I'm just not sure why you thought you could count on him and not yourself."

"I don't know," Spencer said. She hadn't thought about it quite like that. "And now I'm going to have to retake this class, and I don't even know if I need a philosophy class."

"I thought you were planning on minoring in it," Cat said. "Is there a new plan?"

"I don't know," Spencer repeated.

"We can figure it out," Cat said. Spencer nodded. Figuring out things was Cat's favorite hobby. "I mean, what do you want to do?"

Spencer smiled, the sparkle returning to her bloodshot eyes. "Everything. I want to do all of it, Cat."

Cat sighed, but she hugged her roommate and smoothed back her hair. Spencer sank into her shoulder, feeling better than she had in days. Narrowing down her options hurt her head, and now she had more time to figure out which of the countless paths in front of her she wanted to explore. The failed class slid into her past, and dreams of summer shone brightly on the sinking sun.

~

INTERLUDE

SHATTERED MIRROR

My phone buzzes again and again as I sit in the reclined chair, tiny needles injecting toxins into the almost imperceptible wrinkles only my dermatologist and I will ever see. The receptionist discreetly hands me a card on the way out, lowering her eyes as though she doesn't know exactly who I am. Maybe she doesn't care. I'm not the only one who enters this office and says the only prayer I know: *let it keep working*.

The card is unnecessary. My appointments are regular, and my phone chimes with notifications when I need to enter the office to stop time for another few months.

Hopping into a cab, I quickly scan through the text messages, my face either painfully or pleasantly numb; I can't tell the difference anymore. I don't even listen to the voicemails, knowing they're all variations of the same message: *Congratulations on the latest Vogue cover!*

The magazine hasn't even gone to print, but word travels fast in a world where what is current changes by the minute. Bile creeps into my throat as I notice exactly how many messages and texts are flooding into my hand. **Delete all**. I haven't gotten this amount of congratulatory calls in ages, possibly since my first cover too many years ago. September *Vogue* might be considered a coup, but I've been there before.

Anger pushes the bile back into my stomach, shifting into a cold fist of panic and anxiety.

My hands are shaking as I pull my compact out of the ridiculously expensive satchel on the seat beside me. I hold the compact close to my oft-photographed face, turning to let the bright sunlight stream through the dirty filter of the cab window.

Thirty, forty, fifty phone calls congratulating me on something that has been my job, my life, for as long as I can remember, something that wouldn't have been a surprise even two years ago, means only one thing.

Old.

I am getting old.

Staring into the mirror, I can't see any of the panic that fills my insides, a welcome change from the hollow emptiness that comes from years of coffee breakfasts and diet soda lunches. My doctor is unparalleled, perfectly perched on the Botox scale that easily tips from unlined to unmoving, toeing the collagen line that divides the lush from the comical. When I shot my first cover, I never considered letting a needle near the face they were paying me to photograph.

I search the face in the mirror for signs of aging, exhaustion, or gravity. My face, my livelihood, can't calm my anxiety. Only thoughts of the *Vogue* cover, the photo vivid and exquisite in my memory, slow my racing heart. The taxi crawls another few feet and stops, though we're not near a light. At fifteen, the traffic scared me. Now I simply welcome the chance to look, unobserved, at the world outside the grimy window. We're in the midst of brownstones and trendy cafes that allow children to run amok in the interest of collecting all their parents' money.

A broken bouquet balances precariously on the curb, the paper familiar to anyone who wanders past the city's bodegas regularly. They're forgiveness flowers or just because flowers, and for a split second I wonder what they commemorated before being tossed to the ground. I used to get flowers after successful shoots, when I smiled without worrying about lines around my eyes and still treated myself to a latte every so often instead of black coffee, always extra hot.

My phone rings, then stops. Rings again. My agent's ring tone.

There's a problem with the cover, she says. It's not going to run. They're swapping it for a photo from a small shoot they did yesterday morning, with a young model so fresh her head shot's not even on her agency's website. They say her name is Eirwen; she doesn't use a last name.

Carla's voice cajoles and reassures, but I don't hear it. Bile rises again, anxiety flamed into anger once again. I hurl the compact against the window, shattering the mirror. Blood pounds in my ears, mocking me: *old, tired, hag, finished.*

I am twenty-four years old.

∽

SYMBIOSIS

LIBBY

*L*ibby hadn't eaten all day, and even though she was on her way to meet her friend at a new restaurant down the street, the aroma of hot pretzels and street meat convinced her to pause for a quick snack. The pretzel vendor looked bored, of course, as many of them did this time of night. Things would pick up soon, when drunk girls realized they needed carbs to make it through the rest of the bar hours or exhausted lawyers grabbed something to nosh before meeting their takeout delivery in their lobbies.

She'd been stopping at pretzel carts for the last few weeks, the salty, carb-heavy twists settling her stomach and her mind. The last time she'd eaten so much bread she'd been in college, dialing pizza delivery and making ridiculous deals with her roommates about who would have to keep on their bra until the delivery guy arrived. Those days, they'd cobbled together money from their leftover student loans or high-interest credit cards. Now, she dug in her purse for cash, handing over a crumpled hundred-dollar bill with a sigh. She'd actually forgotten about withdrawing it earlier in the week, which was part of the reason her bank balance was in disarray. The vendor shook his head in irritation, counting out the change in a fistful of random bills she didn't check before shoving them back into her bag.

"That looks amazing." The voice came from over her shoulder, and she could tell the words were just as empty as any pickup line she'd heard in a bar.

She turned toward him with the same dismissive smile she wore when dealing with men who expected her to be an associate in her firm instead of a vice president. Self-assured, smiling eyes met her own, though, and she could tell he wasn't the type of man who was used to being dismissed. She idly wondered if he would consider the ring on her finger as a deterrent or a challenge. She quickly noted he didn't wear one of his own.

"It is," she said, sidestepping him without changing her smile in the least.

"I don't suppose there's any chance you'd like to sit for a few minutes and share that with me," he said. His impeccable suit clearly stated he didn't need to share her food for financial reasons, and she was years past being charmed by random men.

"At this point in the day, I wouldn't share this pretzel with my best friend," she said, turning and striding down the street. By the time she was a block away, the encounter was almost forgotten, except for a slight curiosity as to whether he would use that line on anyone else this evening.

"Libby!"

The low-slung table in the lounge area promised a night of carefully angled knees and probably a sore back, but Tiffany had been trying to get reservations for over a month. Libby couldn't remember for the life of her if she'd heard of the chef because of a reality show or because he was dating a Top 40 starlet. She'd been spending so much time at work, she couldn't keep track of which restaurant housed which tabloid darling. Thankfully, water waited for her in a chilled glass, and she gulped half of it before sitting, the ice cubes clicking annoyingly against her teeth.

"Sorry. I stopped for a pretzel on the way. I was absolutely famished."

"I know," Tiffany teased. "Corporate takeovers and columns of numbers and very little time to breathe."

"I've been a mess lately, huh?" Libby gestured to the other poured glass at her place setting. "You can drink the wine, remember?"

"Oh, the baby!" Tiffany widened her eyes. "I completely forgot. I mean, I remembered, but I forgot when I had her pour. It's just that you and I have been getting together for Friday night dinners with wine since…well…forever."

Libby sat, smoothing her dress over an abdomen that still didn't hint at the news she'd only told a handful of people. Her pregnancy hadn't been a surprise or a plan, really. She and Mark had talked about trying for a baby, and she'd had her IUD removed months before, but they both worked such late hours that it almost felt lucky if they were awake at the same time for more than a night or two in a row each month.

"I'm pretty sure I forget about it just as much as you do," Libby teased, but it wasn't the truth at all. She'd been shocked, and a little dismayed actually, with how much she'd fallen in love with the idea of their baby from the moment she realized what her queasy stomach meant.

"Just wait until your ankles start swelling. You won't forget about it when you can't wear your heels anymore."

"I'll be back in them soon enough," Libby said. "I can't command a board meeting in a pair of Ugg boots and yoga pants."

The stereotype fell from her lips without a thought, and she refused to chastise herself for it.

"How much time are you taking off?" Tiffany asked, pulling out her phone and scrolling through the calendar.

Libby looked at her, horrified. "I haven't even considered talking about it at work yet, and you're asking me about maternity leave?"

"You need to plan, Lib. It's not like you get to waltz out of there and waltz back in when the mood strikes."

Libby closed her eyes and reached for the water dripping condensation onto the low table. When she opened them, a waitress stood expectantly. Libby smiled an apology for needing more time, but she couldn't bring herself to peruse the menu.

"How much time off did you take?" she asked, because she felt a little like she was drowning.

"Sixteen weeks with Marcus. Only eleven with Mariana. A huge case came through, and I knew I needed to be a part of it if I wanted any chance at a promotion the following year. Remember how stressed I was about the tariff case?" Tiffany said. Libby ignored the hurt in her friend's face. Tiffany obviously had expected Libby to know all about her maternity leaves, but until she'd seen the positive pregnancy test in her hand—and oh, God, had she really clutched something in her hand that she'd basically peed all over?—pregnancy had been an abstract, her honorary niece and nephew so much more fun since they had started talking and could understand at least a sliver of sarcasm.

"Maybe I can just take off a few weeks and do some work from home. I remember visiting you when Juju was a little nugget, and she slept for the entire visit."

Tiffany rubbed her forehead. "I don't know…maybe…."

Libby could hear the veiled judgment. "You don't think that'll work?"

"With some babies, maybe," Tiffany said. "There's no way to know, though, until you have her."

"Her? How did we move from 'your baby's the size of an almond' to 'her'?" Libby gulped water, glad the pretzel was there to absorb the sloshing feeling in her stomach.

"I have to imagine a force of nature like yourself could only bring forth more estrogen into the world. Lord help poor Aaron."

"Aaron more than holds his own," Libby said, finally opening the menu and running her finger down the creamy ecru paper. Small plates. Perfection.

"I know. He's basically my boss." Tiffany and Libby had been friends almost since birth, their mothers meeting in a music class where new moms desperately sought out friends while their babies tried to cut their teeth on tambourines. Tiffany had introduced Libby to Aaron after meeting him in a law school study group. After graduation, Tiffany and Aaron started at the same firm in the same year.

"Still surreal. You're much too brilliant to be working for Aaron."

Tiffany looked down, lashes shadowing her expressive eyes. "Maybe. I also have to make sure I'm home at a reasonable hour so Natalie doesn't have to ride the subway home in the middle of the night."

Libby shifted uncomfortably at the regret in her friend's voice. She couldn't tell if Tiffany meant she wanted to get home earlier or stay at work later, and she felt awash in guilt that she'd never really considered the question until right now.

Blinking a few times before looking back at Libby, Tiffany sighed. "You might want to start thinking about that, too."

"Riding the subway?"

"Interviewing nannies."

"Christ, Tiff. I only told my parents about it last Tuesday."

"Things are…accelerated when you're talking about

someone who can deal with the hours you work. If you're still going to be working those hours. God. I just realized I never even asked if that's what you planned to do."

Libby coughed on her water. "You're kidding, right? I've figured out a way to squeeze twenty-five hours out of twenty-four hour days for the last ten years. I'm not about to give all that up. Do you plan on asking Aaron if he's going to rearrange his work schedule?"

Silence loomed between them, until one of them filled it with chatter about which small plates to order and laughed about how they needed more with Libby's growing appetite. Tiffany started drinking Libby's glass of wine, and Libby wished for an instant she could let herself fall into the comfortable softness of Pinot Noir, a softness that could smooth away the pity she'd seen in her friend's eyes.

She recognized the look. In fact, Tiffany had been the one to point it out to her when she'd been pregnant with Mariana. With Marcus, pregnancy had been a vast landscape of unknowns, and Tiffany had dived into it with zeal, buying into every sort of information she could digest. By the time Juliette came along, complete with increased morning sickness and decreased sleep, courtesy of a toddler, the glossy sheen had worn off growing a human. *"You'll see. The moms who have been around for a while look at you like you have no clue what you're getting into. I can be holding Marcus on my hip, and someone with a five-year-old is smiling and nodding at me like she's a freaking Oracle and it's all downhill from here."*

Libby resented being on the receiving end of the pity, even more so because it had cracked open a chasm of uncertainty she'd been trying to ignore. She had grown accustomed to sharing her body with this little being, at once an abstraction and her entire world. What would it be like to kiss her goodbye—and now she couldn't help but agree with Tiffany that her baby would be a girl—and jostle for space in the subway before dawn just to get in a little extra work before the trading floor opened for the day? What would it be like when a little voice could ask her not to leave?

At the same time, could she do what Tiffany had done and cradle her infant at home while being leapfrogged for a promotion she'd definitely earned, that she'd clawed and fought for?

Her stomach threatened to rebel against the soft pretzel, and she couldn't tell if it was pregnancy or anxiety causing the roiling. Taking deep breaths, she dug in her purse for some of the peppermints she'd stashed there, grabbing essential oil and dabbing it on her wrist. Seeing her friend struggle, Tiffany reached out to touch her forearm.

"Remember when you used to think you could fight off your nausea or exhaustion with a cigarette and a can of Coke?"

Libby laughed, eyes still watering just a little. "I didn't *think* that. That was a proven remedy."

Tiffany leaned back against the leather banquette. Libby noticed Tiffany's bright red toenails, shoes kicked somewhere under the table, though she still managed to look effortlessly polished after a long day at work.

"Things," Tiffany sighed before gathering her words, "were so much easier to navigate when we only had to worry about beating out the men in our classes for top scores."

Libby slid her own feet out of her shoes and leaned back to mirror her friend. Things might never be that easy again. Automatically, her hand rounded over her belly, and she couldn't remember when she'd picked up that habit.

∼

INTERLUDE

THE LAYOVER

I waved off the driver and dropped our suitcase into the cab's trunk myself. June insisted on keeping her backpack with us, and her faded yellow blanket never left her side while we traveled. It hardly left her side at all. I tried to convince her to leave it in her bed, in part to save my own sanity. Finding her blankie took longer than I could stand at the end of some nights, when I'd wrung out all my patience on reading and homework and constant dusting. She deserved the security, though, especially with a mother like me who wasn't sure what I was doing half the time.

"What are we doing after Niagara Falls again?" June asked. Our itinerary should have been tattooed on her brain by now. She'd been glued to my side as I planned it, her purple glittered fingertips tracing the roads from Niagara Falls upstate. She'd always had an instinct for direction and space, building block structures that awed me, though mostly everything she did awed me, especially since we became a party of two.

"You tell me, buttercup," I said.

"Up, up, up the road to see Grandpa's old cottage on the island," she said, enchanted by the whole idea of visiting a cottage she had never heard about, owned by a man she had never met.

Her eyes sparkled with the magic of the trip, their sea green so much like her father's eyes I had to look away. I pointed to one of the skyscrapers looming over the city, but she was more interested in the bridges, of course, and I let her distract herself with their structure and purpose so she wouldn't notice how far away my thoughts were. Crushed rose petals strewn across the cement caught my eye, and my heart clenched with how forlorn the city seemed when you took the time to notice.

"Why didn't we visit anyone?" June asked, and worry nudged at the base of my spine.

"I don't even know anyone living in the city," I said. I had to be careful with her. She'd inherited my uncanny knack for sniffing out lies, but I could still get away with sliding around the truth if I was careful about revealing just enough to seem like the truth. I often wondered what she would do with that instinct.

"It's weird to come here if we aren't visiting someone," she said, rubbing her blanket against her cheek, a habit she developed in infancy and likely didn't even know she was doing half the time.

"When did you get so smart?" I said. "I thought you might want to see Manhattan."

"The bridges were neat," she said, sighing. "But I don't know if I like cities."

"We live in a city, June bug," I reminded her, though the difference in the energy between New York and San Francisco felt tangible.

"There's more air in ours," June argued.

A picture of my childhood arose, unbidden, the juxtaposition between the open desert neighborhood and the false promises offered by the Vegas strip. Sometimes too much air didn't help things, either.

"Well, there's going to be lots of air near the falls, and even more up on the island," I said.

"And water," June giggled.

"And water," I agreed. I was scrolling through my phone again, hoping I had missed a phone call or text from the person I arranged this layover to see, despite my arguments to the contrary.

I felt foolish. I hadn't spoken with Charlie in years, and I should have known better than to think he would respond well to hearing from me now. His brother's texts were insistent, though, trading in on promises we all made too many years ago, pulling me back to a man I couldn't seem to stop wanting to help.

The last time I tried to help Charlie, he refused, or at least he refused by ignoring my help. Our lives were already diverging, but I sent him a plane ticket, hoping he would understand the implications of what I was offering. I practiced what I'd say to him when he saw my burgeoning belly, my wedding ring growing tight on my left hand. I sat on a bench outside the airport long after he should have arrived, watching weary business travelers and eager tourists stream through the doors to the overcast afternoon. He never came, and I angrily ignored his calls until he stopped making them.

"Do you know I went to Niagara Falls the day I learned I was pregnant with you?" I asked. The memory burned a little. The future had seemed so uncertain, the force of the water pouring into the lake relentless in its movement.

"Was Daddy there?" she asked, and I should have known that would be her question. Scott's accident had happened well before she was able to remember his smile, and she spent her life vacillating between voracious interest in his photos and stories and a happy apathy that came from being raised by a mother singularly devoted to her.

"No, I was actually in New York on business. I traveled so much more before you were born, love."

My phone buzzed as I told her the story, and I jumped a little, willing Charlie's name to pop onto the screen. I tried to ignore the disappointment when I saw it was just my boss, checking in to see when I'd be back in San Francisco. As I was apt to do, I channeled the disappointment into anger, firing off a text to Charlie's brother about Charlie not wanting my help. I wouldn't see his return text until we landed at the small airport in Niagara Falls. I would let the tears fall later that night, when June fell asleep and I worried to myself that missing connections might be the only thing Charlie and I would ever be able to get right.

∼

AT THE TERMINAL

MARGOT

Margot eased her feet out of her heels the moment she sank into the backseat of the cab, wondering too late whether or not her feet would stink up the entire car. Thankfully, she reminded herself, she was in New York, where drivers had likely smelled much worse than her feet. It made her smile to think of what Jaxon, her driver, might have said in Omaha the week before, where she took a private car to and from the airport. Jaxon-with-an-x had told her at least three times he'd had the Town Car detailed the week before. Her brow furrowed. Had that been Omaha? Maybe Kansas City? Airports and hotels and small business conference rooms all ran together after months of travel.

"Heading home?" her current driver asked. She didn't bother to glance at his name. She was too tired to remember anything this afternoon.

"Not yet," Margot said, and she could hear the weariness in her own voice. "One more stop this week."

"For business?"

The questions filled the space between her own

exhausted thoughts, ones she didn't want to consider at the moment. The answers to these filler questions were easier, rote by now, and she could make small talk all the way to the airport if necessary.

"Yes. I train small businesses on software. Really, it's just integrated accounting software, but…." Her voice trailed off. Talking felt a little more strenuous than she'd anticipated. Her driver gave the sort of generic agreement that actually said he understood she didn't want to chat. Thumbing through her confirmation documents on her phone, Margot breathed a sigh of relief that she was traveling west to end the week. She'd finally be able to crawl into bed and get a solid night's sleep—or at least a solid night of flipping back and forth on a too-soft hotel pillow.

Two missed texts from Vance, one asking how training had gone and the second reminding her he had a second, post-dinner meeting and wouldn't be available to chat until late at night. Margot swiped her thumb to a different app, only half-wondering about the late meeting. He'd been taking more and more of them, and though she knew selling was exhausting in a way training wasn't, she was beginning to resent the dinners and laughter she imagined when she was stuck in a conference room or ordering another chicken salad from room service. He was in Chicago right now, which meant she'd be flying over him in just a couple of hours.

Her head hurt.

Leaning against the cool window, she attempted to will her pounding head into submission. The car idled at a light, and she gave herself a little internal high five for scheduling her flight in the early afternoon instead of offering eight hours of training for the last of the three days. She knew the people in her sessions would be glad of the release, and she would be at the airport before the worst of the traffic started—not that Manhattan traffic was ever light.

A bank of blue city rental bikes caught her eye. When she did her last training here, snow had blanketed the city, but she promised herself the next time she landed in New York, she would take one of the bikes for a ride around, even if she just went and cycled through Central Park for a bit. The recirculated air in the office buildings she normally worked took its toll on her sinuses—and her mood, to be honest—after weeks and weeks of shuttling between cities. She hadn't found the time to try out the bikes, of course. She might have even forgotten about them until this group forced her to remember. Averting her eyes, she saw a broken bouquet of roses on the ground. Her stomach clenched at the dozen broken promises strewn next to the one she had made to herself. How many more would she put up with before making a real change?

Another text chimed, but this one made her smile:

Wine at the airport after TSA check?

One of her closest college friends lived in Brooklyn, but they hadn't been able to connect on any of Margot's previous training visits to the city. This time, Kailey was flying back from a ten-day vacation to somewhere tropical; Margot hadn't paid too much attention to the actual destination. All airports had started to look the same about six months ago, and she barely remembered that sometimes those airports were actually gateways to something more than another business opportunity.

Be there as soon as traffic lets me.

Her response was automatic. Talking to a friend face-to-face seemed like a luxury lately. She and Vance only crossed paths at their apartment about five or six days a month, and their social calendar had withered into oblivion. He promised they would start looking for buyers for the company almost a year ago, but booming sales dazzled him until he forgot to notice the lethargic circles under his wife's eyes. Tears pricked at her eyelids, but she squeezed them shut against the impending cry. She'd left her waterproof mascara at some city in the never-ending Midwest, and she didn't feel like redoing her makeup before meeting Kailey.

Stopping the tears worsened the pounding in her head, and she dug in her bag for the tiny bottle of caffeine-laced headache medication. Instead of smooth plastic, her fingers closed on heavy cardstock. She drew it out, her brain unable to place what might be lurking in the bottom of her bag. Margot stared at the once-glossy card she unearthed, and she knew she hadn't dropped it into her bag. Traveling back and forth without going home meant she had gotten quite adept at packing only what she needed, without picking up extraneous bits of ephemera along the way. Flipping to the backside of the card, she saw the jagged black lettering she'd recognize anywhere. She had been reading Vance's jotted notes since he left the first one on her computer screen in a freshman honors class she'd taken for credit and he'd taken for kicks.

> *Heard about this installation from Josh and thought you'd dig it. Check it out Monday night. It won't kill you to be a little tired for a day of training you could pull off in your sleep. xxx*

Regret dug at her gut, chased by a sliver of exasperation. Vance never took the easy route. If he just had mentioned the gallery during one of their conversations, she wouldn't have missed the installation because the card got crushed between a notebook and two half-filled water bottles. Tucking the annoyance into her heart like a shield, she sighed. Whether or not Vance was ready to sell, she was ready to stop schlepping his dream around the country. The problem was she had no idea how to tell him that.

∽

A flurry of texts led Margot to a little wine bar, where Kailey was already noshing on a charcuterie tray. Years fell away in a single hug, and Margot let her bags fall to the ground as she grabbed the wine list from her friend's hand.

"I don't believe it's been three years," Kailey said.

"You look amazing," Margot said, feeling self-conscious about the bags under her eyes and the slightly wrinkled blouse draped over black pants that had seemed so sleek at the beginning of the day.

"Don't let the glow of ten days in paradise fool you," Kailey said. "Before we left I looked like a truck ran over me. I don't know why I expected practicing law to get easier with time. I just seem to get busier."

"I'm pretty sure we both got a one-way ticket to the cult of busyness," Margot said, ordering a dry red and promising herself she would locate that headache medicine she'd gotten distracted from finding in the cab.

"Take a break," Kailey said. "Honestly, I was so ready to just quit everything—including my marriage, if we're being honest—before we went on this vacation."

Margot gulped her wine. She'd forgotten this about Kailey, the open personality that would share absolutely every secret she had with just about anyone who smiled her way. The tumbling words would have gotten her into more skirmishes in their sorority house if Kailey's heart wasn't even bigger than her mouth. She was the first person to defend her friends, take on an extra portion of a project, or to take over a planning committee. Margot's own secrets never seemed to operate the same way; they stayed buried in her sternum, choking her until she could barely breathe.

"I'm so glad it helped," Margot said. The words sounded trite echoing in her head. Had months of limited social interaction caused her to lose all her conversational skills? She tried again. "Do you think it was spending time with Eric or just getting away from the office?"

"Both, I think." Kailey picked up a cracker. "Maybe it was going back to carbs after limiting myself for the better part of a year."

"Did you find it hard to be away from work for so long?"

"Not after the first few days," Kailey said. "We attacked the vacation like we do our jobs: snorkeling, hiking, parasailing. After exhausting ourselves for a couple days, we kind of figured out there was something miraculous about lounge chairs and morning naps."

Margot picked at cheese, swirling a bite of it in the honey drizzled onto the platter. She couldn't remember the last time she and Vance had been together without talking about the business. Even as early as their honeymoon, he'd been making long lists and lofty plans. She'd been all in at that point, of course, loving the idea of building something for themselves that didn't involve working in a cubicle or even a windowed office each day, like so many of their friends had fallen into doing after college.

"You travel all the time, though," Kailey said. "I probably sound ridiculous."

Margot laughed, signaling the bartender for another glass of wine. "What I do isn't anything like snorkeling, beaches, and naps. What you're describing sounds like heaven."

"What you two are doing is amazing, though. Eric and I

were talking about how fabulous it must be to build a successful company on your own terms."

"We're building it on Vance's terms," Margot said. "Not mine."

Kailey blinked, and Margot felt her stomach churn in a mixture of horror and empowerment. She hadn't even said those words to herself.

"I would have sold a year ago, settled down somewhere. But as long as it's growing…."

"But you do so much of the work," Kailey said, furrowing her brow. "Have you thought about hiring someone to do some of the training so you don't have to travel so much?"

"We talked about it maybe six months ago," Margot said, cringing at the thought of that conversation. They priced it out, and Vance had vocally opposed the idea until they were at an impasse. She agreed it made more sense for her to stay in her position, and it did, at least rationally. She was just so tired of living out of her suitcase, even though she bought the brightest one she could find, one that made her smile the first thirty times she pulled it off the luggage carousel.

"I understand," Kailey said. She glanced down, and Margot's eyes followed, pale pink nails standing out prettily against her freshly tanned skin. "I thought about doing public defense work for a while, but if I can tough out working at this firm for the next couple of years…well, we're talking about being in such a better financial position for when we have kids."

Kids. The word barely registered in Margot's head. She and Vance wanted kids. They had talked about kids and timelines in laughing conversations and serious chats long before they even got engaged. The company had taken on a life of its own since then, and now all talk of children had been pushed off to the elusive someday, the day between now and when they would finally sell and settle down. Kids were impossible the way they lived now.

Shocking herself for the second time since she sat down with Kailey, Margot felt her eyes fill with unbidden tears. Kailey's face filled with concern, but her sunny personality and desire to help took over. She handed Margot a couple of cocktail napkins she grabbed from the other side of the bar.

"I'm so sorry if I brought up something you didn't want to talk about. You just always sounded so excited about all of it."

Margot nodded, trying to decide if she trusted her voice yet. "I am. I mean, I was. The software truly does make a difference, especially for small companies. The problem is, all those small companies need separate sales meetings and separate training sessions, and it's all become a little overwhelming when I think about it not having an end in sight."

"Well, then, you'll just have to find that end. There's nothing that says you have to do this forever, even if it's something Vance sees himself continuing indefinitely."

With the words in the air, from someone else's mouth, Margot could see how rational Kailey sounded. After all, she and Vance had built everything together, from the software itself to the original business plan. She had every right in the world, every right in their marriage, to be honest about needing to stop traveling so much. She would tell him the next time they were together.

"You're right." Margot said. She tried the words again. "You're absolutely right. I need to be honest with Vance. And I need to go, or I'm going to miss my plane."

They hugged, Margot squeezing her friend tightly. "No offense, Kailey, but I hope I'm not back in New York for a while."

"Don't say that," Kailey said. "Just come back for a visit instead. I absolutely know how to lounge away the day now."

Margot quickly made her way to the gate. With each step,

her resolve lessened. Away from Kailey, it started to seem a little ridiculous to think she could dictate such a major change about a joint business venture. By the time she sank into the uncomfortable row of chairs to wait for the boarding call, her headache was back with a vengeance. Digging into her bag again, her fingers closed on the smooth plastic, and she drew out the bottle. By the time she wrestled open the childproof cap she would have sworn her headache was worse. Popping two pills in her mouth, Margot stared at the plane sitting at the gate just outside the window. As the acetaminophen kicked in, smoothing out the jagged edges of her pain, she finally breathed. She'd give him six more months.

∼

INTERLUDE

PRO BONO

"That smells amazing," said a voice. The slurred words and haze of Scotch were uncomfortable on my neck, and I spun around with raised eyebrows.

"You sound like you could use something to eat," I said. Drunken men in my personal space were an annoyance, but I doubted this one meant much harm. The ridiculous line about my sandwich sounded like a last-ditch effort to make a connection, though the shawarma was, in fact, mouth-watering. I'd walked out of my way to grab one, because the cart near my office wasn't nearly as savory. Overly white teeth and an expensive haircut would have impressed me five years ago, but I've realized since then that expensive trappings could mask just as much ugliness as bad haircuts and ill-fitting clothes. I walked around him, and my steps were met with exaggerated hands, as though I was the one inconveniencing him.

"I wasn't hitting on you, you know," he called after me, though he obviously had been if he was so eager to explain he wasn't. "I'm engaged. Getting married. I'm actually on the way to…pick up flowers or something for my fiancée."

Confusion lingered in his voice as the sentence trailed into silence. For a moment, I felt for him, wondering what type of woman had coerced this overdressed man into an engagement. By the time the taxi slowed at the curb, I stopped wondering. There were worse things in life than marriage, like the divorce settlements I negotiated daily for people willing to barter away their lives for a bit of freedom.

I shook off expensive divorce settlements by doing pro bono work at the shelter, disentangling women from marriages only holy on paper. Abuse and neglect filled those halls, and I vocally worked to get the women slates as fresh as possible. The conference room negotiations I did for my firm sucked out empathy for my fellow humans, but time at the shelter let it seep back into my soul.

Half of my sandwich remained when I sank into the cab, regretting as I generally did on Fridays that I wasn't taking the subway. I balanced it on my knees as my phone rang, and I could see the driver study me in the mirror, trying to figure out if the circles under my eyes were byproducts of long days or long nights. The director of the shelter speaks into my ear, resolute. One of the women returned home to gather some belongings, something she never should have done, though so many of them do it without incident.

"Leah, she's in the hospital. They don't know if she'll be able to see out of her left eye when the swelling goes down."

My knees sag, and the sandwich falls to the floor of the cab. I'll feel bad about it later, maybe, the garlic sauce pungent on the carpet long after I've paid my fare. Maybe I won't. I used to wonder how the director's voice could be so level, so even, as she recounted horrors over the phone or over the desk in her office. My office at my firm was plush and sterile and designed to inspire confidence. Hers was a janitor's closet, yet I coveted it. My yearly bonuses were tucked firmly into an untouchable account at the bank. A few more years, and I would be able to quit all together and start working at the shelter full-time, maybe running for city council, where I could start making an even greater impact.

I tilted the phone to the side of my mouth as I continued to talk about next steps, letting the driver know I needed to get out of the cab here, now, no matter where I was. My feet knew, right then, I needed to be at that hospital. I needed to be at that shelter, even without the security of a cushy salary and three more years of bonuses. In three years, it might be too late.

∽

ABOVE THE CITY

MAREN AND JULIA

No one in the bar looked at Maren. She was accustomed to her sidekick status; she had been since middle school, when Julia learned the command she had on the stage could be translated to any room into which she walked. Years later, when Drew remarked that Julia's looks were something harder to categorize than beautiful, Maren knew he was right. Julia's magnetism wasn't about beauty. A car accident had dimmed her luster for a while, but Maren hoped to catch glimpses of it again this weekend.

Her flight delayed, she barely had time to drop off her bag before Julia insisted on dragging her out to a sushi place with a longer wait than the security line at the Buffalo airport she just left. Maren hadn't expected Julia to drop Jefferson's last name so cavalierly, leaning onto the sleek hostess stand with her left hand, leading the hostess to shuffle reservations and cut their wait to the time it took to drink a single, overpriced martini.

Several cocktails into the evening, and two dive bars later, Maren had switched to beer and finally felt like she was with her best friend again and not a carbon copy wearing more expensive jeans and less interesting conversation.

"You know what this means," Maren said, scanning the scarred tables and oversized screens. She recognized this bar; not this exact one, but the kind of sports bar she'd been in countless times with her college boyfriend and their friends. They might be in Julia's city, but they were in a place Maren could navigate, maybe someplace she could get her friend to open up about what seemed like a colossal mistake.

"A shot of tequila?" Julia guessed, sucking in her stomach. "I'm going to gain thirty pounds in alcohol alone tonight."

"Not possible, I don't think," Maren said. "But either way, that's not what I meant. I think you and I need to grab one of those trivia machines and show Manhattan exactly how smart we are."

"Maybe you," Julia laughed. "I was lucky to get my GED once I started dancing."

Maren set her jaw. "A piece of paper doesn't define how much you know."

Julia laughed, but Maren heard the hardness buried there. "Philosophy? Is it time to cut you off?"

"Nope. I just don't like hearing you talk like that," Maren said. She thought of her own fine arts degree, gathering dust on a shelf with her unfinished canvases and brushes she hadn't touched in over a year.

"You've always believed in me, Maren. I'm lucky," Julia said.

Maren saw the crack of vulnerability but knew better than to pursue it yet. She hugged her friend instead. "This is getting a little too emotional. Go find the trivia thing, and I'll get shots."

"Perfect," Julia said, and Maren took a moment to admire how Julia parted the crowd simply by walking in a straight line.

Half of the vodka was on the bar floor by the time she got back to their high-top table, and Julia was jabbing at her phone in annoyance. The trivia controller sat in front of her, and she would glance up at the questions and punch the answer with the same amount of annoyance.

"You're about seven times grumpier than when I walked to the bar," Maren said, setting the half-empty shots on the table.

"Did you drink them?" Julia asked, a shadow of a smile coming back into her face.

"Nope. I apparently do better working retail than waiting tables," Maren said.

"Jefferson thinks he should stop by and say hi to you," Julia said, rolling her eyes.

"Is he at your apartment?" Maren said. Disappointment clouded her answer. Jeff had never been anything but kind to her, but she'd been looking forward to a night out with her friend before the craziness of the rest of the weekend.

"No. He's not living there yet, remember? He says he's in the neighborhood though."

"Well, I guess I better order three shots for our next round," Maren said, forcing a smile.

"There's no way he's going to stay here long," Julia said, looking around like she was seeing the bar for the first time.

They answered another three or four questions before Jefferson walked in, and Maren immediately saw what Julia meant. He scanned the bar quickly, saw them and walked quickly to their table, looking like he didn't want to touch anything along the way. His smile didn't reach his eyes, but Maren felt half convinced by it anyway. She blinked hard, wondering if it was the half that was already woozy from the alcohol.

"It's lovely to see you again, Maren," he said, kissing her on the cheek. Maren noticed he tilted his face toward Julia's, but she shifted slightly so his lips hit the corner of her mouth instead of her lips. "Hello, love."

"We were surprised to hear you'd be meeting us," Julia said, her smile twice as kind as her tone.

"I won't stay. I know you've been looking forward to tonight," he said. "I thought I had plans, but I got some unexpected news, so I think I'll just go home."

Maren felt herself relax, and she could see Julia's hands unclench. She tried to remember if she'd ever felt so reluctant to spend time with Drew. He rested his hands on the table for an instant, then withdrew them, maybe when he felt the stickiness of a table that had only been wiped with a day-old bar rag. His head swiveled to Julia's face when he saw what was sitting on the table.

"Trivia?"

"We used to play all the time," Maren said.

"When, exactly?" Jefferson asked. His voice was neutral, but Maren could hear the challenge there, and she wished she wouldn't have said anything. She had played frequently, but Julia hadn't been there during those college weekends that stretched for four days some weeks.

"Your fiancée is actually amazing at it," Maren said, shifting gears.

"It must be nice," he said, turning to Julia, "to have a friend who believes you're fantastic at everything."

Maren knew her own shoulders would have sagged if Drew would have spoken to her like that, but Julia's stick-straight posture didn't waver. In fact, her eyes looked even clearer than they had moments before.

"I'm lucky," she said. "I wouldn't want you to think I don't understand that. Some people might say I'm the luckiest girl in the city."

Maren saw their eyes lock in a steely gaze fighting between attraction and contempt, and her relief escaped in an audible sigh when she saw attraction win. Jefferson tilted his forehead to Julia's, and this time she didn't shy away from his kiss.

"It's going to be okay, right, J?" His question dropped to a whisper, and Maren felt like she was eavesdropping.

"I'm not sure anymore, J. I hope so," Julia answered. She blinked hard as he walked away, and Maren recognized the gesture. Julia had perfected the containment of tears before she'd left Buffalo for Manhattan, and she hadn't changed her technique since then.

Knowing her head would be pounding in the morning either way, Maren took one of the shots remaining on the table, and Julia wordlessly did the same. Not knowing if she could stand a conversation with Julia that didn't include what was happening with Jefferson, Maren did the only thing she could think of. She took Julia's hand and led her to the dance floor, if you could call the tiny square in front of a sagging DJ booth a stage.

"You know I don't dance any—"

"Tonight, you do. Tonight you dance."

Maren dug her toes into the plush carpet lining the dressing room floor. She couldn't remember the last time she'd changed in a stall with better carpet than her parent's house, one that looked as though someone ran a vacuum cleaner over its lush expanse at least three times a day. She'd taken off her shoes by habit, curling her legs underneath her and leaning into the corner of the mirror while she waited for Julia to return from yet another lap around the sales floor. At least three saleswomen had offered to help, but Jules had waved them away from the room with an icy dismissal Maren didn't recognize.

Maren thought of fifty places she'd rather be: Drew's tiny apartment within spitting distance from the law library; her favorite treadmill at the gym; the bar she and Julia had doubled over in laughter at the night before. None of them made much sense, she argued with herself. Clothes were one of the vestiges she clung to as a form of expression since she'd given up painting—taken a break, really, though she admitted to Julia that she couldn't imagine touching a brush in the near future. Maybe not in any future. The softly lit slip dresses and starkly geometric pants should have thrilled her, but something about the carpet felt suffocating.

"I'm back." Julia bumped open the door with a hip too slim to be considered a curve. Dresses covered both her arms, Champagne flutes precariously gripped in both hands. Thankful for something tangible to do, Maren grabbed the delicate glasses and placed them on a teensy table in the corner. She felt better knowing the incongruous table served a purpose after all.

"I'm bearing gifts, but the Champagne might be the best one," Julia sighed, picking up the flute and gesturing for Maren to do the same.

Accustomed to the grimy beer mugs at college bars, Maren's fingers weren't quite sure where to rest on the thin-as-air stem. She did, however, recognize the glitter in Julia's eyes that meant clinking the glasses together was the best move she could make. Maren didn't know much about wine, but the cloying sweetness on her tongue filled her mouth in a way that reminded her of the cheap bubbly wine that lined counters of every New Year's Eve party she'd ever attended. Strangely, knowing the store was serving something cheap in their fancy glasses centered her.

"Jules. I brought three dresses with me. One of them should work," Maren said. She'd mentioned that to Julia, of course, more than once, but the dresses still sat in the closet of a brownstone where even Julia barely knew her way around.

"I want to buy you something," Julia said. "It's the least I can do for interrupting Drew right before finals. And, after all, I'm only going to have one engagement party."

The tension in the air blossomed. Maren still couldn't believe the heavy ring weighing down her friend's hand. Half the time she wasn't sure Julia believed it either, though she certainly seemed to believe in the slim, black piece of plastic she'd wielded with impunity the last two days.

"Not true. I'm counting last night as your first engagement party," Maren said, testing how much of her friend might remain beneath the frantic yet icy facade.

Julia's familiar laugh echoed off the tastefully papered walls, and Maren relaxed enough to take a full drink of the bubbly wine tickling her nose. Julia drank, too, and scrunched up her fine-boned face in distaste.

"You're so right, Mare. That should count as my engagement party! No one but you would talk me into trivia and dancing on a postage-sized, sticky dance floor in the same night. This is terrible Champagne."

"Definitely purchased in bulk from the bottom shelf, and of course I provided the most entertaining party in the city. No one but me knows how much irrelevant knowledge you have tucked away in that brain of yours," Maren said.

Julia nodded, and Maren thought she saw her friend's jaw clench for just an instant. "I'm afraid you might be right about that."

To avoid Julia's eyes, Maren hung up the dresses Julia had tossed across the fitting room chair, smoothing fabric and taking note of price tags. When she glanced on the four-digit cost of a deceptively simple lace sheath, she dropped it as though burned.

"Julia. I can't."

"Try it on at least," Julia said. Her own hands trailed across the fabric as if she was only truly seeing it with the sensitive tips of her fingers. "I told you it's my treat. Well, Jeff's treat, but he would be the first person to notice if you weren't wearing what he deemed the right thing, so he won't mind."

Maren pulled her t-shirt over her head and pulled on the dress, unwillingly charmed by the way the fabric skimmed across her body. The lining shimmered, adding dimension and a slight edge to the delicate lace.

Julia leaned against the wall, her calculated stare making Maren feel like one of the canvases she appraised at the museum. Despite her unexpected want for the dress she'd shunned moments before, she was grateful when Jules nodded her approval and she could shrug on her favorite tee.

"What are you wearing, by the way?" Maren asked. "You told me you'd show me after the bar last night, and then…."

"We kicked butt in bar trivia and you insisted on lemon drops and a terribly executed dance party."

"Guilty," Maren said, "but I still deserve to see your dress, since you basically decided none of mine were suitable for this shindig."

Julia pulled out her phone, scrolling through photos until she found the one she wanted, a dark, glittering dress that looked dangerously close to one of the costumes she'd worn as a ballerina. Sleeker than a costume, the dress managed to be eye-catching without mocking Julia's former career. Still, Maren felt unease with the choice.

"Well, one thing Jefferson's brought out in you is better taste in clothes," Maren said, swallowing the remainder of her champagne in a single gulp.

Julia's nod seemed sage rather than joyful. "He's nothing if not concerned with the way everything looks, you know. There are so many days I feel like a diamond he's polishing."

Maren pulled on her jeans and let the pause between them grow.

"I thought it would feel better," Julia said. "The polishing, I mean. I thought it would feel more like love."

Maren handed the dress to her oldest friend, the one whose wedding she would have agreed to stand up in if Julia was marrying Satan incarnate. Julia's engagement had been splashed around society columns since it had been carefully announced. The ring and the reservation at the Plaza and the brownstone into which she'd already moved were envy inducing, especially to Maren's college friends.

Now, looking into Julia's eyes and seeing how many more glasses of Champagne it might take before she laughed again, Maren didn't feel jealous. She simply felt like crying. Instead, she hung the impossibly expensive dress on the hanger on the door, pressing it gently against the wood.

"I think I might let Jefferson buy me this dress after all." Maren felt a savage flash of resentment toward the man she'd found basically charming during each of their meetings. "And Jules? You don't need to be polished."

Julia's intake of breath felt like a confession, but the moment dissolved as one of their phones chimed and they remembered there was a party waiting in a few hours, somewhere where all the plush carpet in the world couldn't cushion the train wreck that seemed to have already left the station.

∼

"Is there anyone I absolutely need to remember?" Maren asked, her eyes slightly hazy from the bottle of Champagne the friends had finished as the afternoon light slid into dusk. "I want to perform my maid of honor duties in stellar fashion."

"Jefferson, of course," Julia giggled, pushing aside the sadness she thought she glimpsed in Maren's eyes. The party would be painful enough without her oldest friend acting like they were attending a funeral instead.

"When is he moving in again?" Maren asked, hip checking Julia away from the full-length mirror. They were both in Julia's closet, if you could call it a closet. Maren had declared it larger than the bedrooms in her childhood home. Makeup littered the sleek cabinet island, and Julia felt like she might be able to close her eyes and will herself back to the crowded college apartment where she'd visited Maren during her friend's undergraduate years. She let her memories linger on Maren's place; her own tiny, shared studio bursting with pointe shoes and drip-dried tights belonged in another lifetime.

"He still has his other apartment until the end of the year," Julia said. She didn't mind having the expansive brownstone unit to herself for a while. Everywhere else in the city felt claustrophobic since she'd agreed to Jeff's proposal. Photos appeared when she hadn't known they were taken, and people she only met in passing were so effusive in their praise that she felt both more invisible and completely exposed with each day. Hedge fund managers didn't normally warrant space on paparazzi hard drives, but his politically-connected family, combined with her former stage career, made them more interesting as a couple than they'd ever been as individuals. "Speaking of living with attractive men, what's happening with you and Mr. Drew?"

"I'm not moving into that apartment," Maren said, wrinkling her nose. "And he doesn't want to leave until he graduates."

"Which happens in what? A month?" Julia said.

"Who else should I know besides your fiancé?" Maren asked, smoothing down the dress they purchased earlier in the day. Feeling the dismissal, Julia pressed her fingers against her head, fighting away the headache that lingered constantly. She knew she had pressured Maren into the dress, but her future mother-in-law would have loved to drop a couple well-timed barbs about any of the dresses Maren had brought along from Buffalo. Even with Maren's impeccable taste, Jefferson's mother could smell something mass-produced from a mile away.

"You'll want to keep a wide berth from Jefferson's mother once you make polite conversation for a few minutes. Jeff will do his best to keep her in check tonight, but she's an expert at sussing out embarrassing information and tucking it away until she can use it like a sword," Julia said, surprising herself with her candor.

The slight buzz cleared from Maren's eyes, and she looked nervous.

"I'm out of my league here, Jules," she said.

"I probably am, too, Mare. But you've got to admit it'll be fascinating to see how the second act of my life unfolds."

Strings of fairy lights turned the roof of the brownstone into something like magic, but Julia couldn't help wondering what sort of stars would be visible if she could get away from the lights of the city. She managed to glide amongst the guests without truly talking to any of them, her conversations as light and bubbly as the Champagne she grasped at all times. She learned to do it with her right hand, the better to leave her left free to be pawed and fawned over. Julia wasn't sure if she was imagining the way her future mother-in-law's eyes seemed glued to the ring on her hand, but she found herself flitting and twirling to corners and groups of people who could shield her from the icy gaze.

"I saw you dance once, you know," a woman said, blue eyes warm with admiration in a perfectly forgettable face.

Julia felt her lips forming a vague sort of response. Words didn't exist to bridge the gap between where she once imagined she would be and this softly lit rooftop. Stories and stories below, cars stopped and started at lights, veering around each other, near misses and guardian angels keeping the dreams of their passengers intact for another night. Her right toes ached, stilettos keeping her feet firmly encased in shoes that reminded her she'd never take the stage again.

"I'm just so pleased to be in a position where I can still support the ballet world," Julia said. The answer was practiced, designed as a shield against the agonizing reaction she had whenever someone mentioned her former career.

Jeff circled back to her periodically, sliding an arm around her waist, kissing her temple, and occasionally nuzzling her neck. Julia measured the liquor he drank by the warmth in his eyes and tried to push down her irritation with his impeccably timed returns. He excelled at public appearances.

"Of course The Plaza," he said to the small cluster of people surrounding the couple. "Mother insisted, as you might imagine."

Julia smiled on cue, letting her head fall back to look up at her fiancé. He winked at her and leaned down to whisper in her ear. She braced herself, but his mood was still celebratory.

"Can you imagine Mother's reaction if she knew I floated the idea of an elopement the night I asked for your lovely hand in marriage?"

Julia relaxed against him for a moment. He had opened the velvet-lined box in a rush, and she knew he had a different proposal in mind when the words tumbled out in a convoluted speech about making their own way in his parents' world. Their excitement over their unchartered future led them to share dreams and fears neither had spoken until that night. But in the morning, the words seemed far away. They commenced their careful hops between dots his mother outlined for them during a staid dinner where she never even said congratulations. By the end of that dinner, Julia could barely breathe, and she wondered if she would ever again see the Jefferson who whispered the world to her with hope in his eyes.

"What a dream," a voice gushed. Julia met the eyes of a women she vaguely remembered meeting earlier in the night, a newly married wife of someone in Jeff's firm. The gushing words didn't meet the cool eyes staring back at Julia, and she extricated herself from Jeff's embrace. She needed air. Panic almost resulted in laughter as she looked around. There wasn't a place in New York with more available air than a rooftop.

A subtle gleam of expensive fabric caught her eye, and Julia changed her path to find the one safe haven in the entire party. Maren and Drew stood on the periphery of the party, near a table cluttered with glasses of wine and appetizers people seemed to be staring at but not touching. Julia noticed her friend, however, had a full plate of food—or as full as one could make a cocktail-hour plate. Even though her friends welcomed her with a smile, Julia felt as though she was intruding.

"Stunning setup, Jules," Maren said.

Julia nodded, feeling her throat close in gratitude at the slightly deprecating tone in Maren's voice.

"I had very little to do with it, of course," she said, reaching for another glass of wine. She couldn't remember how many she'd started to sip before abandoning each of them on side tables and trays, the glasses whisked away before she noticed by waiters with white gloves and silent feet.

"Of course. Why would you want to plan your own engagement party?"

"Jeff's mother has a very definite idea of how this marriage should be executed," Julia said. The words sounded more bitter than she expected. After all, she was the one who insisted to Jeff that she was more than happy to acquiesce to his mother's particular ideas.

"I'm sure she does," Maren said. Silence buffered her words, and Julia bristled against the concern she heard there.

"Don't. Please."

"You, of all people, know she's not going to stop until she says what she needs to say," Drew said. His voice was layered with apology, admiration, and the bare kind of love he couldn't hide behind his nonchalance.

"I guess I just don't understand why any of this is happening," Maren said.

"Luck?" Julia said.

"Maybe for someone," Maren admitted. "Snagging Jefferson off the trust fund bachelor registry would have been a coup for a lot of girls."

"Not for me?" Julia asked, her tone deceptively light. "What makes me so different?"

"We all know you weren't looking for someone to take care of you," Maren said.

Julia found herself unable to meet Maren's eyes. When she was with her friend, she felt almost invincible, almost the way she felt the first time she had auditioned. Her feet always knew exactly what to do. She hadn't yet learned to exert the same kind of control over her life.

"I wasn't exactly looking for anything that's happened in the last sixteen months," Julia said.

"I know." Maren's words pressed into Julia. Maren was the

only one who had seen Julia cry since the accident, the only one with even a whisper of the anguish that surrounded her. "But you don't need to sign away the rest of your life so soon. Especially not with someone I'm not even sure you like, let alone love."

Julia tightened her grip on the wine glass in her hand. She wanted to shatter it against the brick wall, to grind the stem into sandy shards of glass that could be taken away on a gust of wind. She wanted to turn herself into the same sort of sand, able to escape on a breeze. But what she wanted had proved to be as fragile as her bones had been between the collapsing metal that pinned her foot and leg between the seat and the accordion-like door.

"Do you remember when I met him?" Julia asked. Turning had always been one of her strengths.

Maren nodded.

"He was betting against the Yankees. More money than I'd ever seen, not that I had any idea at the time. I just knew he was the only person in the bar who wanted them to lose."

She saw the defiance in his eyes from where she sat, three seats away at a wooden bar soaked with years of spilled drinks and regret. She smiled because of the defiance, wondering why he looked close to furious even while he clapped with the rest of the bar's patrons when the New York batter hit a game-tying home run. When she walked past him to the bathroom, she willed away her still-recovering limp through gritted teeth. The anger in his eyes had abated the second time she smiled at him, but the defiance lingered, and Julia was almost positive he never would have asked her to join him at the late-night diner if she had been watching the game with her girlfriends and not the achingly earnest doctor she'd been casually dating.

"I don't know if I can get behind you marrying someone who doesn't root for the Yankees," Drew said. Maren's withering look stopped him from taking the joke any further.

Julia narrowed her gaze. "It's not even that he doesn't root for them," she said. "He just likes to be able to say he appreciates an underdog."

"You're not an underdog," Maren said. "What happened to you is awful, but—"

"What happened to me," Julia said, ice in her voice, "was everything. There's nothing after the accident. Nothing else matters."

"Dancing doesn't make you who you are."

"Dancing does," Julia said. "And if I can't do it in front of a crowd, I'll do it in the gorgeous, glittering world Jeff's building for me. I'll twirl for him until I bleed the way my feet used to bleed."

Maren didn't speak. Julia noticed her friend's hand snaking into Drew's, and regret bubbled into her gut before she could tamp it into submission. For the first time in days, she welcomed the sight of Jeff walking toward her. A haze of Scotch introduced his state of mind a heartbeat before he was close enough to speak quietly.

"Mother's looking for you. She means to introduce you to some of the ladies with whom you'll be working on some charity board or another."

Too many fingers of Scotch had chased the defiance from his eyes and left contempt in its wake. Julia braced herself as he swung his arm from behind his back with a flourish. Maren and Drew faded into nothingness next to her as Julia waited for his challenge. He thrust a bodega bouquet of red roses into her chest.

"I ran downstairs to grab these for you," he said. "I know you've always gotten flowers for your most impressive performances."

Her mind cast back, searching for the memory of the first

bouquet Jefferson had bought her: sunny daisies. He explained they were opposite her typical roses because he wanted the two of them to start new traditions together. One day she would let herself sit down and figure out exactly when everything changed, but life had moved in fast-forward since he placed the icy ring on her hand. For tonight Julia wrapped her hand around the bundled stems, holding her breath against the fragrance that had punctuated her most beloved memories. She wouldn't let him taint those for her, though she was more than willing to sacrifice her future to the cool ambition in his eyes. She had forgotten how hard it could be to hold a dozen roses in one hand. The weight was inconsequential, but the girth stretched her fingers. She wouldn't have to hold them for long.

She forced a smile on her face as she flung the flowers away from her, launching them over the side of the roof. From the corner of her eye, she saw Maren and Drew lean over the side of the building to watch the bundled roses careen toward the ground. Only briefly did she wonder what would become of them when they met the unyielding concrete so many feet beneath them.

"This? Consider it a dress rehearsal for the rest of our lives," Julia said.

She ached to look back at her friends, to reassure them with a glance, but she didn't dare. Placing the wine glass on the table, she walked toward Jefferson's mother pushing away the fleeting thought that the weight of the flowers was nothing compared to the heavy promise extending to the knuckle of the third finger on her left hand.

INTERLUDE

IN THE RAIN

Rose pulled neat white gloves over her fingers. She had taken to wearing them about two months ago, aware of the cartoonish look they lent to her retro-heavy wardrobe. Her mother had sighed in resignation after she wore them three times to the country club, though one sniffy octogenarian loudly approved of a return to more modest dressing. She told her mother it had to do with flattering her curves, and that part was true, but there was something else, a quiet kind of rebellion about flaunting not fitting in when she had been given every advantage in the world to have the opportunity to do so.

Joe despised the gloves, of course, though he pretended he appreciated her quirkiness. Rose was fairly certain he resented it. Maybe he'd always resented it, but after he changed jobs to work at the bank instead of the non-profit he fell into after graduation, he'd barely been able to hide his disdain. Each time he made an offhand comment about sleek, trendy clothes, she dug in her heels and trolled another vintage store for something new to wear.

She loved working where she did, where they had both

worked and where they met, and where they started dating after a few too many happy hours that no one else attended because so many of their co-workers couldn't afford to get away with toiling at their non-profit passion project without working another job.

"How d'you do it?" Joe had asked, three martinis into a Friday night, the only time a question like that could be asked.

"Do what?" she asked, pretending not to know, though she had fielded the question before. Her last name wasn't one with which most people were unfamiliar. A quick Google search would shine a light on exactly how she could work where she wanted without a second job, but certain types of people liked to hear it for themselves.

"Save the world without waiting on schmucks like Brando most nights?" Joe's words were slurred, but his revelation wasn't new. She'd already learned how much he resented their boss, how much he resented working for far less than some of his friends who scored meteoric jobs after graduation. She hadn't known then how much he resented that she'd been born into the life he desperately wanted to inhabit.

"I don't have school loans," she hedged, before slugging back half of her fourth martini and ignoring the calculation in his eyes. Instead she focused on how much those eyes looked like the olives in their chilled glasses, and surely the fact that they both drank super dirty martinis meant something more than a penchant for salt.

"So that might explain how you've gotten away with a solitary job, but I don't know if it explains how you're living without anyone else in an actual one-bedroom and not a shitty studio."

His brazen questioning actually made her feel a little bold about her answer, though later she wished she'd met him before Chelsea moved out of their small apartment. Having a roommate might have quelled the probe, at least a little bit. Instead she dropped the phrase "a little family money" neatly into the conversation the way she dropped the cocktail pick back into her glass. Later, her best friend, happily married and comfortably settled, got furious on Rose's behalf.

"Like it's any of his business," she fumed. "He's not working another job, either. He's just living off credit cards. Don't let him live off your money, too."

Rose wanted to feel furious for herself, but it was getting tiring being utterly alone in a world that wanted her to be with someone. With anyone really, which was maybe why Joe had seemed appealing at the beginning.

He at least had the restraint to wait until the following week to kiss her into breathlessness after the happiest happy hour she could remember.

Her *little bit of family money* changed his lifestyle for the better, until he began to want to change hers, mainly the way she dressed and the way she smiled. Her mother, of course, expressed her horror at the way Rose lessened herself in Joe's presence. Rose didn't need to marry, her mother reminded her, as if they were flitting through the 1800s. She never considered that maybe her daughter was aching for a life not defined by cool financial freedom.

She and Joe started to look at co-ops together, traipsing through neighborhoods that bored her on Saturday afternoons. He never mentioned marriage, but he expressed interest in the ornate emerald that rested on her mother's finger. The history of the family ring impressed him, and she supposed there was a miserly bent to the questions. If he even deigned to propose, he could do it without dropping a dime on a ring. Rose hated emeralds, but her words never stuck, and soon she stopped mentioning it. Bit by bit, she quieted herself—at least until she purchased her first pair of gloves on a whim in a vintage store where she'd been hunting for cut glass doorknobs.

This Saturday they were meeting at a cafe he said was halfway between their offices, though of course by the time she made the trek uptown she realized it was a few blocks from his office and an eternity from hers. The gloves came off halfway through her walk, when she felt her fingers start to dampen with perspiration against the pristine fabric. Her hair would frizz before she arrived, and there wasn't much she could do about the sheen of dampness above her lip except for a bit of powder, but she wanted her gloves to be neat when he walked in and saw her at the table. She imagined herself on the patio, gloved fingers folded on the table, a small pot of tea steaming into the air that wasn't quite warm enough to be called balmy. In her imagination, she looked a lot more like a tiara-clad Audrey Hepburn than an erstwhile Eliza Doolittle, all glasses and untamed hair and very little poise, no matter how hard she tried.

Before she even crossed the street to the cafe, she saw that Joe was waiting at a table. The light seemed stuck on red, and she shuffled her feet in her Mary Janes, surprised to see shocking red petals under the black heels. Bouquets weren't anything special in New York, but a shower of abandoned petals tugged her into aching romanticism. She wished Joe would look up and meet her eyes across the street, lean over the wrought iron patio barricade to kiss her into breathlessness again. Instead, she found herself following a bored hostess through the restaurant to the patio door, pulling on the gloves only moments before she walked through the doorway to the outdoors.

"We need," he said, crossing one ankle atop the other knee in an affected leg cross, "to talk."

Rose knew the tone, just like she knew he never could have afforded those loafers he was wearing if they hadn't been a Christmas gift from her. Her breath caught somewhere in her chest, and she fleetingly wondered if her shallow breaths were flattering in the deep, sweetheart neckline.

"Do we?" She might be gawky, and she might be three steps behind in every dating game she ever played, but she had learned the impeccable shield of icy propriety and wielded it even when she wanted to dissolve into the ground.

"I care for you, Rose. You know that."

"Of course," she agreed.

"Our future, though…." He let his voice trail, and she forced herself not to fill the space with an apologetic concession.

Savage satisfaction sent a shiver down her spine when she noted the bead of sweat gathering at his temple. He wiped at it and then rubbed his lips. She would survive this. She always did.

"I just don't see myself with someone who doesn't have any ambition," he said.

She laughed.

Anger flashed in his eyes. His only ambition involved a Bergdorf's card while hers leaned toward the intangible wisps of doing something…anything, really, helpful for the people who hadn't had her advantages. Still, she wouldn't let herself think about the warm way their hands had fit together, the way they had wandered through Central Park without any destination before he decided he could do better than an average woman with an above-average bank account.

Ozone introduced the drops before they fell. It usually did, she knew, though she ignored it every time it happened. Walkers scrambled into doorways or groped for umbrellas in totes. She sank to the undersized chair, while he stood, cursing and shaking rain from his shoulders. With her hair already ruined by humidity, sitting in the rain wouldn't affect her.

Rose watched him walk away from their table with a spine straightened by his revelation. Closing her eyes, she turned her face to the gunmetal clouds and let the sky's tears mingle with her own. The waiter offered her a table inside, but she declined. Later she would wrap herself in a plush towel and sleep away her sadness, but for now she would let the fat raindrops help her say goodbye.

∼

CHASING STROLLERS

NORA

Nora still brought the stroller when they walked, even though Josie would only sit in it for seconds at a time. It had bothered her at first, how slow their daily outings went without Josie contained. Nora's legs didn't remember how to move at a toddler's pace, and she'd feel impatience and embarrassment collide until tears sprang into her eyes. Matt laughed them away.

"Nora, love, what did you think it would mean to raise her here? That she'd pick up the ability to speed walk before she even learned how to write her name?"

"I hate feeling like we're in the way," Nora countered.

"You're always in someone's way here," he said. "It's part of the city's inexplicable charm, the way you annoy the people around you just by existing."

She laughed, the way she always did when Matt buffered her from the loneliness of spending all her time with a little person who mostly talked about stuffed animals and tea parties. His generously poured mimosas helped, too, but Nora hadn't stopped wishing Josie would walk more quickly until the day she started running, threading through the crowd like a torpedo.

Nora abandoned the stroller to chase her daughter, both of them a little shocked when she finally caught Josie and promptly burst into tears. Throngs of people had pushed the stroller to the side, one wheel caught in a sidewalk crack, spinning helplessly. Josie rode home that day, the clatter of the wheels against the concrete lulling her to sleep in a way it hadn't in almost a year, and Nora resigned herself to living in a perpetual state of legs moving too quickly or too slowly.

One day she noticed she didn't feel embarrassed anymore. Josie still stopped just as frequently to look at twinkling chunks of broken glass or the way weeds poked through the sidewalk, but Nora simply planted her feet on both sides of her child, letting walkers stream around her. They grumbled, but Nora no longer heard the words because she concentrated on Josie's burgeoning vocabulary. But she still toted along the stroller, just in case.

"Mama, we go get a cookie today?" Josie asked hopefully, staring out the window one afternoon after a particularly productive nap.

"No, sweets. Remember we talked about not eating giant cookies every day? Besides, I'm fairly sure a certain little girl didn't eat any of her carrots or her broccoli at lunch."

Josie's eyes widened as her nose crinkled. A huge sigh escaped her lungs, and Nora tried not to laugh as Josie pushed her hair back from her face with both palms. She knew the gesture intimately, her own hands pushed her own hair back from her face in exactly the same way.

"Mama. Boppy never eats her carrots, and she can have cookies seven times a day," Josie said.

Boppy didn't protest, the worn elephant half-stuffed under Josie's pillow.

"Maybe Boppy would like to walk over to the playground, even without a cookie," Nora suggested. Their daily walks were as much a part of their routine as tapas-style meals and the nap Josie recently started protesting. Even in rain and snow they tramped around for a few blocks, though on the snowiest days Nora would leave the stroller home. They never went far enough to risk getting stuck in the snow.

"Sure, Mama," Josie agreed.

She plucked Boppy from the pillow and snuggled him into her face before nuzzling Nora's face with the over-loved fur. Nausea swept through Nora's body, sweat beading on her forehead. Her stomach had protested almost everything she touched the last few days, and apparently a utilitarian lunch of chicken salad and Nora's leftover veggies wasn't faring well. She scrambled to the bathroom near Nora's nursery, vowing to toss Boppy in the washer with the next load of clothes so he'd be fresh and ready for bedtime snuggles.

"What're you doing?" Josie demanded, face scrunched in a mix of uncertainty, worry, and distaste.

"Mama's not feeling well," Nora said. She cringed at the way she addressed herself in the third person. She hadn't spoken like that to Josie in what seemed like an eternity, those early years of constant vocabulary building fading away into hazy memories.

"You want to hold Boppy?" Josie held out the elephant, though she looked more than relieved when Nora shook her head. "Missuz Lodi would get you a tube."

Nora felt laughter bubbling behind her ribs, competing with her roiling stomach for attention. "Mrs. Lodi, indeed, would likely have an essential oil roller for Ma—for me. I'm okay now, Sweets. Let's get to the park and swing."

∼

Two hours later, Nora leaned against the back of the park bench, careful not to let the splintery wood poke too closely to her skin. She felt like leaving but wondered if her legs would get her safely back to their apartment. Josie continued her loop around the play structure, a glaze of little girl sweat and dirt plastering curls to her temples. Nora let her neck rest against the back of the bench. If only she could close her eyes for just a moment. All of her conviction that they lived in a safe neighborhood wouldn't allow her to fall prey to the song of sunshine and sleepiness.

"Mama!" Josie's voice cut through the fog of exhaustion.

"Yes, Jojo?"

"I think I want a snack now," Josie said, eyes fixed on the pretzel vendor near the entrance to the park.

She had said no to the cookie idea, but even Nora didn't think she could resist the lure of salt and warm bread mere footsteps away. Josie lofted herself onto the bench beside her mother as Nora dug in her small messenger bag for cash. Her eyes snagged on a mother near the swings, digging through a behemoth of a tote. Nora remembered those days, when she carried around a bag spilling diapers and sippy cups. A thought niggled in her skull, disquieting her, but she turned back to her daughter with a crumpled ten-dollar bill in her hand.

"Do you think you might share your giant pretzel with me?" Nora asked.

Josie nodded and planted a kiss on Nora's nose. "Thanks, Mama!"

Nora inhaled Josie's scent: earth, warmth, and peach-scented shampoo Josie chose based on how much she liked the bottle. The stroller rolled in front of her with one hand, while she tucked Josie's fingers into the palm of her other. Josie's confident voice negotiated the exchange of food for money, but Nora held the pretzel in her own hand, weaving the stroller toward the other side of the cart. Instinctively, she grabbed the mustard, prepared to smear a bit onto her half of the warm pretzel, but the wafting scent turned her stomach again. Almost as if on cue, a baby down the block began to cry, and bits and pieces of the last six weeks slid into place like tumblers clicking in a lock.

She barely remembered their walk home, except for the freedom she felt walking with her child's hand in hers and the stroller in the other, her untouched pretzel nestled in napkins on the seat of the stroller.

A lifetime later, Matt walked through the door. He closed it quietly, but even the subtle noise startled her into consciousness from where she'd fallen asleep on the couch. She dodged his tie as he leaned over to kiss her hello, the cigarettes he pretended not to smoke reminding her of a time when they'd wander to the sidewalk outside of bars and talk until they forgot to go back inside.

"Did you and Jojo try that new yoga class today?"

"No, that's not until next week. Just the park today." Her voice didn't relay the panic circling her brain. "Josie just had leftovers for dinner. Do you want to call for something?"

He sank next to her on the small sofa, and she slid her finger under the loosened tie, reading his day by the deepness of the furrows in his brow, and watching his eyes trail to the edge of the cluttered ottoman.

"Why's the baby monitor out here?" They hadn't needed it once they discovered Josie wouldn't spontaneously combust if they didn't watch each moment of her nap.

She had almost forgotten taking Josie with her to ransack their small storage area after dinner.

"It doesn't work anymore," she started.

He nodded, his patience calming her worry, but only slightly.

"I'm pregnant," she blurted.

He blinked, and then a smile cracked open his face.

"I didn't even realize it was a possibility right now," he said. His arms circled her, lips pressed against her forehead. She could feel the steady thud of his heart and tried to concentrate on its rhythm. Everything in her own body felt foreign and off-kilter.

"I'm pregnant, and our baby monitor doesn't even work," she said.

Laughter rumbled in his chest. "So we'll get a new monitor," he started, but his voice changed when he saw the brightness of tears in her eyes. "Oh, hey, Nor. This is a good thing, isn't it?"

"Yes?" She couldn't make her answer anything other than a question.

"I know we haven't talked about it in a while, but I always thought…"

"No. I know. I mean, we never planned on having Josie be our only child. I'm just scared shitless I won't be able to make this work, you know?"

Confusion battled with excitement in his face, and part of her hated she hadn't come to terms with the pregnancy before tossing it into the space between them. But she'd never hidden anything from him, especially not something that affected both of them irrevocably.

"What do you mean, love? You're a killer mom."

"I'm her mom, though, and I barely have that figured out. How am I supposed to push her stroller and hold a baby and carry a damn diaper bag again?"

He sighed, just enough for her to hear and she backpedaled a little. "I'm not suggesting we leave the city. I know you don't want to do that, and I don't even want to do that anymore, but...."

"But you're kind of suggesting it?" The probing question was gentler than she expected, a contrast to the heated arguments they had about it for months after Josie started crawling, shrinking their apartment into minuscule proportions.

His chest had always been the most comfortable place to rest, and she couldn't bring herself to look into his eyes quite yet.

"I don't know," she admitted.

"Listen, love, we don't have to decide anything tonight," he said. She could hear the smoothness of his voice, the one she always imagined he used during his most explosive client meetings, but she was too exhausted to worry she was being placated.

"Let's get tacos," she said. "I can't think of anything that sounds good to eat except a vat of guacamole."

He grinned, smoothing back her hair.

"We're having another baby," he said. She let the seed of his excitement bury itself in her chest and take bloom, just a smidge. She kept her eyes off the hallway, where the doors would remind her of Josie's small room and the even smaller third bedroom that was scarcely more than a closet.

Matt was gone by the time she woke the next morning, her alarm quietly chiming her to life so she could make coffee before her daughter's chatter overwhelmed her day. He left a text for her from the train, a few words reminding her of how thrilled he was about their news.

Her single brewer worked its magic quickly, and she lazily wondered if the caffeine recommendations for pregnant women had changed since her last pregnancy. Instead of a quick Internet search that might make her feel guilty, she liberally poured flavored creamer and sipped in ignorant bliss for at least one more day. A moment later, she heard tiny feet hit the ground running, and she felt claustrophobia threaten as she imagined a crib geometrically wedged into the sparse space in which they lived.

"Morning, Jojo," she said, peppering her daughter's unruly curls with kisses. "Let's go get an egg sandwich from the deli."

Josie looked delighted with the unexpected treat, and they both dressed quickly. Nora imagined she felt a swelling under the waistband of her favorite jeans already, but she shook her head at herself. Right now the only thing she wanted to do was get out of the apartment and get a little bit of air.

On the sidewalk, she immediately worried she'd made a mistake. The bustle of commuters still clogged the streets, and she felt Josie's fingers pulling her forward through the ocean of people. Instead of fresh air, she felt assaulted by expensive perfume and gourmet coffee steaming from familiar white cups that had once been ubiquitously cardboard.

Only steps from the crosswalk, Josie stopped abruptly. Almost on top of her daughter, Nora looked down. Josie had assumed one of her favorite positions, crouched over the sidewalk, hands splayed on her knees as she keenly observed a cluster of rose petals on the ground. Even Nora felt drawn to them, red satin ovals tumbled onto the concrete in small clusters. Before she could stop Josie, the little girl scooped a bunch of them between her hands and stood, pressing them toward Nora.

"Look Mama! I found you some flowers," she said.

Nora let herself inhale their perfume.

Josie clapped her hands in excitement, and the petals drifted back to the ground.

"I always find such beautiful things when we walk." Josie's sigh of contentment sounded exactly like Matt, and Nora knew, somehow, their baby would fit into their city life just perfectly.

∼

INTERLUDE

THE TULIPS

Lucy had purchased a practical trench coat the first week she moved to the city. For longer than she could remember, she'd coveted the iconic plaid lining, and she believed it was a felicitous sign that she found one in a thrift shop the first time she wandered through those particular doors. Her mother's countless fashion magazines promised a better life through high-end fashion, and Lucy knew it must be true. The glossy covers hid their treasures inside, but she brought them to the light, tearing out her favorites and lining the vanity mirror where she practiced finding the exact shade of lip liner that would plump her lips without seeming too obvious.

The trench was the right coat for hailing a cab. She knew it in her bones, though her meager salary meant cab rides were a luxury she could ill afford. She had whiled away the afternoon in the used bookstore, though, and there was no way she would make it back to the office before the end of the day if she attempted the subway. Thankfully, her little excursion had actually been her boss's idea. He wanted to reach out to small businesses in the area, and nowhere did they fail as quickly as they did where the business models were out priced by rising overhead costs.

Her foot brushed against something as she prepared to step off the curb into the street. Green stems poked out of a battered bouquet covering, and she was struck with the romanticism of the city before she noticed none of the blossoms were still attached to their stems.

Looking at it like that felt a little too lonely for Lucy, and she quickly concocted a story about how the bouquet must have been dropped by two lovers embracing after running into each other at the corner, though their rendezvous point was supposed to be somewhere more picturesque, like the bridge at Central Park. Lucy knew that if she were to arrange a meeting with a lover, it would be somewhere near the bridge at Central Park. Three cabs sped past while she reconciled the broken flowers with her perception of the city.

When one finally stopped, she stumbled climbing into it, bumping her head and probably flashing half the walkers on the street, if any of them had been paying any attention. Trying to blink away the stars in her head, Lucy gave the address she needed to be and sank into the cracked backseat. She'd spent almost all of the money she had left for the week on this cab ride, and she wanted to enjoy it. By the time she stepped out onto the sidewalk in front of the looming office building, her head had cleared. With a couple bills clutched in her hand, she paused in front of a bodega.

Roses were too romantic for the office, but the pink and yellow tulips were just the thing to brighten the receptionist desk. They'd wilt soon, of course, but they would be so perfect for the few days they stood at attention for anyone walking into the office. One of her glossy magazines wrote that a penny would perk up cut tulips, and even she could spare a cent or two if it meant another few days of sunshine. She buried her face in the blooms as she waited for the elevator. The rickety car opened, and she blushed when she almost ran directly into her boss.

"Oh! Mr. Walker, I didn't expect to see you here!"

He looked amused. "And I definitely didn't expect to see you here, dear."

"I went over to that bookstore you recommended, and I wanted to type up my report to have it ready for you in the morning," she said.

"Well, thank you for your diligence, Lucy. But you don't need to come into the office on a Sunday for something like that."

Lucy blushed even more deeply. "I'm sorry, sir. I just…."

"Don't worry about it, dear. Do you have plans for dinner? I'm sure Iris would be more than happy to add you to our table. Both boys are eating an early dinner before heading back to college after a weekend at home."

"That would be wonderful," Lucy breathed. Sunday dinners were the loneliest in her little apartment, her roommate gone for most weekends, tucked snugly into her boyfriend's life. "I should probably put these in water, though, before we go."

"Bring them with you, dear. Tulips are my Iris's favorite. I'll reimburse you for them, of course."

Lucy beamed. Maybe, just maybe, the city was less lonely than she thought.

∾

THE INSTALLATION

GENEVIEVE

I snapped and unsnapped my umbrella, unsure if the drizzle dampening my hair was going to turn into full-fledged rain. My feet moved forward of their own accord, as if they remembered how to walk the city streets even though I felt painfully overwhelmed, over stimulated, and completely out of place. When Mitchell and I had contemplated stretching our dollars into the suburbs, we promised each other we would make it a habit to come into the city as much as possible. Now, though, with work intruding on almost all of his waking hours, and my volunteer activities taking over mine, we were infrequent guests at best, taking in shows on weekend nights and checking restaurant reviews before making reservations. The energy of the city had fueled my heartbeat since I walked into my dorm room at NYU, and now I breathed somewhere else, again relegated to outsider status.

A quick glance at my watch told me I had hours left before I had to be home. After a tearful conversation about overlapping extracurricular commitments, Mitchell had encouraged me to call our old nanny to see if Amy could help us out one afternoon a week. I wanted to be grateful for the reprieve, but when I thought of the indulgent way he had chuckled, I felt something more like resentment than appreciation. Today, though, with the overcast promise of spring making me glad I'd grabbed my umbrella, the empty hours remaining in my day felt like a gift.

I had come into the city for something related to the kids, of course. Broadway tickets were always a big-ticket item at the annual school auction. The theaters offered electronic versions of the tickets, but the heavy cardboard could be packaged more prettily, and pretty packaging went a long way at the Westchester elementary school the kids attended. I shook my head a little at that. After so many years of diapers and music classes, preschool days that seemed to be five minutes long between drop off and pick up, it felt a little surreal to have all three kids in one building for a full day of school.

After my meeting, I'd meant to wander aimlessly, but I had forgotten the frantic energy flowing down the sidewalks. Without direction, I was swept away to an area in which I hadn't expected to find myself. The corner, like so many corners, teemed with energy. Contemplating a midday cocktail, I sighed with the weight of a long night of homework and gymnastics gossip and crossed to the opposite corner to push open the door to the tiny cafe.

Coffee would be a better choice.

Unaccustomed to ordering something at an unfamiliar counter, I hesitated.

"A ven—a large Americano, please," I requested.

"I can bring it to your table if you're staying." The barista's bored voice made it clear he didn't want to stray too far from the espresso machine, so I shook my head and leaned against the scarred wood counter to wait. The warm scent of cream and hazelnut tempted, but I'd finally noticed my jeans feeling less tight and I didn't want to undo my early morning runs. I waited for the oversized mug and dumped in several packets of artificial sugar. Mitchell kept harping on the latest research about their safety, but I refused to give up the bit of sweetness I allowed myself each day.

Sinking into the table felt decadent, even without one of the pastries glistening in the glass case. I'd taken an early train, and no one would need me until well after they were done with school, with Amy shuttling the twins to their practices and entertaining the baby—I couldn't get over the fact that my baby was in kindergarten—until I made it home. I almost reached for my phone, wondering what I would see flooding my social media streams this Tuesday, but I forced myself to keep it snugly in my bag and grabbed the glossy magazine instead. I bought it on impulse as I wandered, feeling like I was getting away with something.

I meant to flip idly. Lovely things still seemed more real on the slick pages of a magazine than they did on a screen, no matter how many upgrades I went through on my devices. But as I passed a section on must-see places in the city, my eye snagged on a space I knew better than my own laundry room.

Sun Always Shines in Raindrops on Roses!

I ignored the attempt at a cheeky headline and scanned the text under the photo:

> Shop owner and furniture designer Caroline Cameron meshes unique finds with repurposed furniture in this eclectic boutique. You'll feel like a friend has invited you into her living room—a friend that lets you take home your favorite décor pieces! The inviting and

> irreverent Cameron welcomes the chance to talk about the story behind each of the pieces. She's also available for interior design consulting if you can't figure out how to bring together your own space.

Tears threatened, and my fingers itched for my phone again, but I couldn't call Caroline just yet. Why hadn't Caro mentioned the feature? Though I had walked away from Raindrops on Roses soon after having the twins, Caroline knew how much the store still meant to me. I sighed. Caroline probably hadn't thought I would even see the slim column in a monthly magazine when I could barely return phone calls without scheduling time in my bloated calendar. Still, we texted more than most teenagers. She could have at least mentioned it.

"Genna?" The question shook me out of my head. No one had called me that in years.

I forgot all about crying when I saw the wide smile and sparkling eyes that mirrored my own surprise. My cheeks burned when I saw who was standing above me, even as my fingers stayed pressed against the picture of Caroline's shop, two pieces of my past colliding at one tiny cafe table.

I took a breath to speak, but it caught in my throat and I wished I had ordered a cup of water to go with my coffee. A couple of convulsive swallows helped, but I still didn't have any idea what to say. I thought for an instant that he might turn and leave, that maybe it was all a figment of my imagination, but he broke the silence.

"So, this is surreal," he said.

The last time I heard his voice, there had been derision

and dismissal there, a world of hurt exploding into a final fight. He was leaving for Colorado, for a different life, and I deleted his contact information from my phone, computer, and memory in an attempt to move forward without him in mine.

"That feels like an understatement."

"I didn't even know you were still in the city," he said. "I was on the store's mailing list for a while, and then I wasn't, and you aren't as easy to find as I expected."

My stomach twisted in a way that hovered between hurt and pleasure. I hadn't expected him to ever want to find me. "I'm not exactly still in the city," I said, no idea how much of my life to reveal to him.

"Can I sit?" he asked. I nodded, drowning in my own curiosity.

"Are you visiting?" I asked. I scrolled through old memories, trying to recall what I knew about his closest friends. Some of them must still be here. New York did that to people, cradled her chosen ones until they didn't know how to live anywhere else.

His smile came easily, crinkling the corners of his eyes, and I couldn't help the clutch of my heart when I thought about how beautifully he'd aged. Fifteen years felt like a hundred when I looked at my own face in the mirror, but a thread of silver at his temples and a few crow's feet were the only marks of time I could see on his face.

"Actually I've been back for a couple of years. It turns out it's not as easy to get out of the city as I thought."

My house in the suburbs, the sprawling yard and en suite bathrooms, felt like an affront against his statement. I couldn't tell if I wanted to defend my choice to leave or denounce my entry into SUV ownership. Either way, my life shone in contrast to the person he'd known.

"My dad's still importing coffee, and believe it or not, he asked me to come back and help him with the financials."

"What about the brewery?" I asked. I cringed a little that I knew about it.

"Lonnie got it in the divorce," he said. The word spun like a top in my brain. I hadn't known he was married, let alone divorced, and the gulf between past and present swelled to uncertain proportions. "What about you? I know about the kids," he said. "I think that's when I unsubscribed from the Raindrops on Roses newsletter."

I remembered how easily he slid into that wry tone, the way it felt like a combination of a caress and a challenge, and I felt unsettled that I wanted to hear it again. Falling back into rhythm with him felt intimate—and a little intoxicating.

"I don't know if I ever expected to see you again," I said, the words more a confession than a conversation. For months after he left, I would see him everywhere: men on the subway, dirty Yankees ball caps atop heads in poorly lit bars, customers walking into the store to the cheeky ringing of the bell Caroline had insisted on hanging. Mitchell had vanquished those phantom men, making me laugh until the emptiness from Will's absence faded into something warm and comfortable.

"Some things are inevitable," he said, shrugging. I bristled at that.

"Inevitability is a fallacy."

His low laughter rumbled in his chest. "You haven't changed, have you?"

I had, in a million minuscule and monumental ways, and I tried to remember the ways he had made me feel smaller than I was instead of the way his smile made me feel only moments before. He must have sensed the shift in energy, because he leaned against the table, lessening the space between us. I could smell his cologne and hated myself for wanting to inhale.

"That was supposed to be a compliment, Genna," he said. "Since I've been back it seems like everything I knew has shifted in inexplicable ways."

I remembered this, too, his ability to smooth his words when they didn't go the way he anticipated.

"Fifteen years is a lifetime in some ways," I said, feeling the weight of my family press against my chest.

"And a minute in others," he said. "Can I buy you another coffee? Are you leaving soon?"

I should have said no and yes, but I accepted his offer instead, glancing at my phone and calculating which train I could catch home without taking advantage of Amy's time.

"Do you still drink it black?" he asked when he returned, offering me a steaming mug.

"Sometimes," I said. I hadn't for years, letting the amount of cream creep up and up. I was working on breaking the habit, though, scaling it back on the weekends and cutting it out entirely during the week, working against time to balance my slowing metabolism.

"Are you still digging for buried treasures?" he asked. I had forgotten how he described what Caroline and I did at antique shows and old barns. He never really believed in the store, not even when we secured the loan to open it. He left before we even started renovating the storefront, never saw the way the light made the scarred wooden floors—and our vision—come alive.

"Not really," I said, trying to make it sound like something I'd given up happily. I had, for a while anyway. Only when Logan started preschool had the sacrifice seemed like such and not like the gift it was when Mitchell first admitted my time might be better used at home. I wanted, so badly, to stay with the kids that I hadn't anticipated how it would feel each day they needed me a little less.

"Maybe you should start again," he teased. "You never know what you might find out there."

∼

I gave Will my number in a heady moment where I felt twenty-one again. Somewhere between the florescent lighting in the train station and the scent of tacos wafting from my familiar kitchen, I lost the connection to that fearless version of myself. When his name buzzed my phone to life on the lacquered dining room table of the school's PTA president, I scrambled to grab the slim case. His name meant nothing to anyone in the room but me, yet I could feel guilt creeping rosily into my cheeks.

No one batted an eye. Pings and buzzing and interrupted conversations pieced together the backdrop of our days. I flipped the phone over casually without looking to see what his message said.

An accusatory glance slid my way anyway. I knew Botox wouldn't allow Allie's brow to furrow my way, but it wasn't for lack of trying.

"I can't believe you're leaving us, Gen. There's no one who can run the auction the way you do," Allie said. Her nail, as shiny as the wood table it tapped, slid a copy of my email in my direction, as though I would refute writing it.

"I'm not leaving, Allie," I said. I tried not to sigh. Mitch laughed when I suggested pulling back from my volunteer opportunities would lead to strife, but he didn't understand the school politics the way I did.

"Of course you are," she said. "Stepping down as chair? We have countless hands willing to help with the fundraiser. You know that. We need someone to chair it. We need *you* to chair it."

Allie didn't blink as she poured another inch of Prosecco into my glass. Meetings at Allie's always lead to at least a single glass of wine, though rarely more than that unless she'd decided to forego afternoon Pilates. People talked of Allie's courtroom dominance in her pre-PTA life, and I believed it as I fidgeted slightly with the stem on the wine glass.

"I just…it took up so much time this year," I said. The words felt slightly ridiculous, and Allie jumped on them.

"I understand it's a lot," she said, lowering her voice into the conspiratorial tone that was supposed to put us on the same side. "I thought about stepping away from a couple of my committees last year."

I inhaled and sipped at the wine, regretting the smoothie I left unfinished on my kitchen counter. My head felt a little light already.

"I don't think I can imagine the school running without you," I said. I wasn't sure it was a compliment, but her face relaxed into a smile.

"Well, I don't know about that," she said. "But I do know James suggested I talk to the firm about going back to work part-time."

My head swiveled at her statement. I couldn't picture her in anything other than sleek athletic wear or impeccably trendy gala gear. Maybe she could still surprise me after all.

"I didn't know you were considering that," I said. My phone buzzed again, a pause, and then another vibration.

My interest waned when I heard the horror in her voice.

"Well, I wasn't. I'm not sure what he was thinking," she said. "And you should keep that in mind. If you aren't getting things done at school, what exactly do you plan on doing?"

In the city anytime soon? Let's grab another coffee.

"It's not about me," I lied. "I just think it might be helpful to have some fresh eyes on the project."

She drained the glass in her hand and stood up. The dismissal stung, but not as much as I might have expected a few months ago. I kissed her on the cheek before I left, but I could already see her thoughts casting forward to the next person who would sit in my chair and secure yet another banner year of moneymaking for a school that never really needed it.

What about tomorrow?

I fired off the text before overthinking my answer. While driving, I composed other answers in my head, answers to Allie's question. Without school commitments crowding my calendar, I could do a million things. I could talk to the ancient owner of the antique store a few blocks from here to see if he wanted help. I could run a marathon. I could travel with Mitchell and leave the kids with Amy for a long weekend. My phone pinged in the cup holder not holding my eco-friendly glass water bottle.

Perfect. See you around 10.

I could have coffee with someone who didn't know enough about my life to give me a guilt trip about wanting to change it.

∼

I saw him before he saw me, waiting outside the coffee shop when I arrived. Mirrored aviators hid my surprise, but his own dark sunglasses hid his gaze, too, and I could only imagine his motivation when he asked if I could walk a couple blocks to his brownstone to pick up a package he needed to take to the post office.

"I meant to grab it on the way out, of course," he said. "But I didn't want to be late."

I hadn't answered, measuring the distance between having coffee and entering the home of a man I once wanted so desperately I hadn't been able to articulate the desire even to myself. But if the detour to his place had been contrived, he'd recalculated, suggesting it would be quicker if he ran upstairs himself. He held up a small package and two bottles of water.

"Want to sit for a second?"

I sent up a silent moment of gratitude for my treadmill. Six months ago, I wouldn't have been able to sink down to sit on the cement steps with any semblance of grace. Now, at least, I could fold my legs to the side and tuck my practical leather tote between the iron rail and the faded red brick wall. Will sat, too, pocketing his keys and leaning against the wall. He belonged there, not caring about the discomfort of the bricks when all I could think about was whether they'd snag the oversized cashmere sweater that was perfectly on-trend but too heavy for the oppressive heat snaking its way into the city.

"I'm sure you don't smoke anymore," he said, producing a pack of cigarettes from his pocket. I remembered, inexplicably, that his smokes always appeared like this, palmed in his left hand, the scent of tobacco wafting from a slightly crumpled pack.

I could see Will knew the answer already, so I didn't bother to lie.

"No. I don't," I said. I slid my hand toward his anyway, my

eyes holding his gaze as he shook the slim cylinder into my waiting palm.

I rolled it between my fingers, amazed at how naturally my hand lifted it up to my lips, how perfectly I remembered how to breathe in just enough over the flame flickering at the end of his lighter.

I inhaled deeply, not caring that it burned my lungs. Nicotine buzzed in my veins, and I couldn't tell if it was breaking down a barrier or putting up a shield. His eyes glued to mine, but I couldn't read anything there and looked away. The impenetrable shine of my polished nails felt safer, so I stared at them and smoked. The pale pink looked out of place against the cement stoop, and I pressed my fingers against it to see the contrast.

My hands looked like my mother's, thin and pale, though I knew she'd never be sitting here, staring at the way her engagement ring caught the sun into prisms across from a man she'd last seen as a boy. The cigarette smoldered slowly, and it felt like a luxury. Traffic idled on the street in front of us, nameless faces who couldn't care less who sat on the corner stoop. The anonymity felt more luxurious than the cigarette, and I didn't hesitate to accept a second when the first burned down almost to my fingers.

I could feel Will biding his time silently, and I braced myself when he drew in his breath to speak. His questions should have shattered the air between us, and I was ready to guard against anything he might ask. Instead, he slid his phone across the stoop. Even as I sat across from him, stolen minutes ticking in the back of my heart, I couldn't help but notice his slim phone wasn't encased in the familiar protective casing used by nearly everyone I knew. The chasm between his life and mine seemed as simple—and complicated—as the industrial cover protecting my own phone from sticky fingers that dropped it each time they touched it.

"I wasn't sure you'd come," he said, his words cementing the deliberateness of my arrival. "But I thought if you did, we could go check out this exhibit."

I barely glanced at his phone before my stomach clenched in a sort of betrayal. Will had kissed me once on a stoop like this, in a part of town where shabbiness was a reality and not a choice. His lips on mine, right now, with my wedding ring sparkling in the sun wouldn't have seemed as intimate as what he proposed. I stared at the website glowing from the screen, trying to think of the last time I'd been to an evening event without Mitch or the gaggle of moms from the kids' school.

"I can't remember the last time I went to a gallery opening."

I could, of course, and that was part of the problem. Caroline and I had made plans to see a photography series, one Caroline thought about bringing into the store, a combination of original pieces and printed copies of the work. The abandoned farmhouses fit perfectly with the aesthetic Caro and I had curated for years. They ended up being the perfect backdrop for Caroline's fallen—but relieved—expression when I admitted I needed time away from work to take care of my brood of babies.

"Huh. You used to relish finding new places, new people," he said, voice neutral. I couldn't tell if his expression was curiosity or pity, and I crushed the remainder of the cigarette under the expensively shabby block heel of my boots.

"There's not as much of an opportunity in…." My voice trailed off. My rationalizations didn't mean anything here, not with a man who didn't know my children, hadn't seen the way their faces lit up when I walked through the door of their classrooms.

He plucked his phone from my grasp. I desperately wanted the universe to give me a sign about what I was supposed to do, but I was fairly sure I'd have to be the one to make this leap on my own. I didn't have to study the website to know the opening would be under the cover of darkness, when I had no real excuse for wandering into the city and leaving Amy in charge of bedtime and the hours until Mitch returned from work.

"Let's do it," I said, a savage sort of rebellion tasting like acid in my throat.

His smile danced in his eyes, and I folded my hands together, twisting the stone in my ring into my palm, like that somehow negated its presence, like Will wasn't entirely aware of its existence.

"Perfect. We can meet here, if that works for you. It's a short walk," he said, gesturing vaguely up the street. He pulled a glossy postcard from his back pocket and pressed it into my hand. I couldn't tell if it was warm from being tucked so close to his body or if I was projecting meaning onto everything in hopes of making sense of the tumbling emotions that refused to settle enough for me to interpret what they actually meant. "I grabbed this for you, so you don't forget."

I nodded with a shrug, like it wasn't a decision that might change everything. Dizzy with nicotine and uncertainty, I stood, acting as though I needed to leave, though I'd only just arrived. He stood, too, his eyes holding me in an embrace his arms didn't attempt. I bounced my feet down the steps before turning to walk back to the subway station. I pushed through the turnstile before realizing we hadn't returned to the coffee shop at all.

∽

"You're never going to guess who I ran into a few weeks ago," I said. I concentrated on the French press in front of me, no matter that even my kindergartner could press a stopper against a bunch of coffee grounds.

"That doesn't narrow it down at all," Caroline said.

"I was in the city getting tickets for the kids' silent auction, and I also happened to see that article about Raindrops on Roses…." I poured coffee into two oversized mugs and immediately starting boiling another pot of water.

"I thought we talked that topic to death," Caroline said, opening and closing the flavored creamer three times before sighing and pouring a liberal stream into her steaming cup.

I tried not to bristle at Caroline's tone. We had talked in circles, and I embarrassingly cried over wine. I shouldn't blame my happily married, completely childless friend for moving forward with a career we dreamt up together during late night study sessions when we were finished cramming but too wired to consider sleeping.

"Anyway, I was looking at the article and wondering why you decided to wear something floral after I constantly tell you to always photograph in sapphire at the store," I said.

"You're right about that. I saw it as soon as the piece dropped. I looked like I was hiding behind some cushion I picked up at an estate sale and forgot to repurpose," Caroline said. "And it's going to be a puffy cushion if I don't break this addiction to chocolate mint creamer."

Our banter felt so familiar and so easy. I almost regretted what I was about to say to Caroline, but it already hurt that I'd kept the secret for so long. After all, I had texted Caroline approximately fourteen times a day since that day in the city, and I never mentioned seeing Will, let alone any of our other meetings.

"So it seemed like some sort of kismet that I'm reading an article that always makes me think of those nights in college, and Will walks over to my table."

Caroline started coughing. "Wait. Will? I thought he was

somewhere in Portland, growing weed and regressing a little more each year?"

"Colorado, not Portland. And all of that seems to have been a little exaggerated," I said.

"What the—Gen, why do you sound like you're defending him? I was actually glad he was morphing into some disappearing pot guru. I kicked him out of our house fifteen years ago, and I'd do it again."

"He's back in the city because his dad needed help with their business. They do those trophies every Little League coach in the world gives to the kids at the end of each season?"

"You picked up a lot of information in the coffee shop," Caroline said, narrowing her eyes in my direction.

"Well, that's the other thing," I said, sipping my own coffee gingerly. Without any creamer, it took longer to cool to a temperate that wouldn't burn my tongue, but I wasn't sure how to segue into the rest of the conversation.

"Genevieve Walker. By the time you get out whatever secret you have hidden under that perfectly messy bun, your kids are going to be here, and I'm going to have to be the fun aunt and give them each a phone so they'll leave us alone to finish this conversation."

"It wasn't just one conversation in a coffee shop," I said.

"By that, you mean you got up to go to the bathroom, and then you had a second conversation. Maybe got a bagel to let him know you might look good right now, but you're ready to puff out with carbs at a moment's notice?"

"Thanks for the vote of confidence in my carb avoidance," I said.

"Like hell this is about carbs," Caroline bit back.

"We've met for coffee a couple more times," I said, balancing the truth with a vagueness surrounding the number. Four times. Five if you counted the time we never made it to the coffee shop and drank water on his stoop.

Caroline narrowed her eyes, and I felt her bore into every conversation we'd had about relationships, the ones from the near past all the way back to the ones about boys we liked well before we had any idea about how heartbreaking liking boys could be.

"And?"

"Maybe a little visit to the Met one afternoon," I said.

"So what you're telling me is you're having an affair with a man who shattered everything fifteen years ago."

"Don't be insane."

Caroline glowered, and I started again.

"I'm not having an affair. This has nothing to do with Mitchell and me," I said the words, knowing they didn't have the conviction they should have.

"What do you mean it hasn't got anything to do with your husband? Unless, of course, he's completely aware of all of these jaunts to the city."

"He's perfectly aware of my jaunts to the city," I said. My face flamed, hot and uncomfortable, and I felt my anger edging toward tears. "He's the one who encouraged me to get out more, to do something more with my time than just hover around the kids at school."

"I don't think he expected you to start dating," Caroline said.

I dropped the French press carafe, shattering it in the sink. Caroline jumped to her feet, words tumbling on top of each other, while she gently cradled my hands to look for cuts.

"I'm being a bitch," she said. "I believe you. And it's not like, even if you were having an affair, that you're cheating on me."

I absently picked up the largest pieces of glass to drop into the recycling containers neatly concealed behind wood cabinet fronts in the kitchen island. Caroline shooed me away to one of the stools and cleaned up the rest of the shards.

"Do you have another one?" she asked. "I know you can't handle life without a cup of coffee firmly in hand."

"I've got at least two back-up caffeine sources," I said. Hearing the judgment drain from Caroline's voice released some of the air stuck in my chest.

"Tell me more about this," Caroline said.

"The bad thing, Caro? Honest to God. I was more nervous about telling you than if Mitch would have asked me about it."

"That's because I once threatened to shave his lying head," Caroline said lightly. "Mitch only experienced the aftermath of Will."

"It's not that, though. It's that he's so busy and so distracted, I really don't know if he would feel rage or relief. Something to keep me busy might be exactly the thing to let him feel a little less guilty about not coming home for more than ten hours each week."

"Oh, hon. That's not true, and you know it. A Pilates addiction might make him feel a little better, maybe, but he doesn't want to drift apart that way."

I took a breath. I wanted to admit to Caroline that I worried we had been adrift for a while, but I couldn't voice that, not even to my best friend. Some words, I knew, couldn't be put back inside once they were outside your heart. I still wanted Caroline to look at Mitch with the same exasperated affection she had since she met him and found out he was a Mets fan.

"I know it's going to end badly," I said.

"What does that mean, though?" Caroline asked. "There's a million ways it could end."

"I think that's the problem," I said. "I'm just not sure."

∼

The twins were reading in their rooms when I heard tiny feet padding down the stairs. Logan had never understood the concept of staying in his bedroom after Mitch and I said goodnight. He starting climbing, half-catapulting himself out of his crib long before we were planning to move him into a real bed, and even when we child-proofed his door, we would find him with a blanket on the floor in the morning, sometimes near his bookshelf, other times next to open drawers, where he'd obviously fallen asleep while removing every pair of socks he could find. Eventually, we grew accustomed to his wake ups, little footsteps, and obscure questions.

"Hi, Mommy," he said, and I could see the sleep threatening to take over his heavy-lidded hazel eyes. I once expected they would be my own amber, but like the twins, Mitch's green had crept into his orbs.

"Hey, baby. You look pretty sleepy. What's going on?"

"I was worried about something," he said. My hands flexed in exasperation, and guilt flooded through my body to the tips of my fingers. Logan was always worried about something. The word didn't mean the same thing to him as it did to the rest of us. He meant "wondering" most of the time, but I found it sweetly charming and hadn't wanted to correct him. Now, though, I was the worried one, concerned he noticed a shift in my attention, a disruption in the air around the house.

"Is there a question I can answer for you?" I asked, pulling him into my arms. He sank onto the couch next to me, curling into my side like a much younger child.

"You went to the city again," he said, and I breathed

deeply, forcing myself to leave my wine on the wooden tray in front of me.

"Why are you worried about the city?"

"Well, when Aunt Caro was here she said I could have one of those candies from her store," Logan said. "And you didn't bring me one home."

I relaxed, pulling him a little closer. "Oh, buddy. I didn't go to the store this time."

"But why? It's my favorite place in the whole city. Maybe the whole world," Logan said. I smothered laughter. From the countless colorful trinkets to the oversized jar of rock candy on the counter, Caroline never shied the kids away from interacting with anything on her shelves, no matter how worried I felt about them crashing around like small, clumsy elephants.

"I know, Logan. I just had something else to do today." Something that had become a habit—conversations at a table by the window. We wandered to the Met only once, and the vulnerability of walking through something so beautiful with him had almost scared me from meeting him again. Almost.

"Maybe we could go soon," Logan said. "I really want to get a blue candy this time. Oli told me it will turn my tongue *blue*."

"Oliver's probably right about that."

"I worry it might stay blue," Logan said, "but I still have to try it."

I sighed. I could, more than I wanted to admit, understand the compulsion to try something with a major potential downside. "I think I like your tongue exactly the way it is, Logan-bear. But candy only makes it blue for a little while, not forever."

He tucked his head more firmly under my chin, and I breathed in the clean scent of fresh shampoo and exhaustion.

"Then let's go to Aunt Caro's soon," he decided. "Can you take me back upstairs, Mommy?"

"There's nothing I'd rather be doing," I said, and the truth of my words hit me so hard I almost couldn't breathe. I slung him onto my hip, though his legs dangled dangerously close to my knees. My back swayed to balance his growing weight. He grew heavier with each step, and by the time I restarted his nightlight and smoothed his hair back with a soft hand and softer song, he was struggling to keep his eyes open.

I heard Mitch come into the house and silently willed him to stay downstairs for a few minutes until Logan fell asleep. Both of them would be disappointed to know they had barely missed a father-son goodnight, but Mitch's arrival would result in at least fifteen more worries and wonders from our constantly-thinking boy. Peeking into the other bedrooms, I found Oliver and Charlotte both asleep with their books open on their chest. Oli's was a tattered choose-your-adventure paperback he found at the used bookstore, and I yearned to finger through it on my own. I'd never been good at reading those for pleasure; I'd keep my finger firmly in each fork in the story, wanting the ability to take back the choice I made if it didn't turn out the way I expected.

"I didn't expect you home so early," I said when I finally met Mitch in the living room. I hesitated before walking toward him for our customary welcome-home embrace, and for a moment my self-loathing eclipsed the feeling of contentment Logan had elicited only minutes before. Shaking my head, I walked toward my husband anyway. His tie had been tossed into his bag at some point during the day, and I buried my nose into his slightly-wrinkled shirtfront, so familiar with the smell of the detergent that it felt like home.

His kiss on my temple burned into my consciousness. He stepped away to pour his own glass of wine from the open bottle on the already wiped down kitchen island. Automatically, I felt a little resentment that he was probably going to want some sort of dinner, and I'd have to wipe down the counter for the four hundred and seventy-first time that day.

Mitch surprised me.

"They catered in dinner," he said, nodding toward the living room. "Today was insanity, and all I want to do is put up my feet for a few minutes and hear what you've been up to. I mean, you just referred to nine o'clock at night as early, and that seems crazy, Gen."

"It's crazy," I agreed. The words were as automatic as the flash of resentment, but I felt their truth as I followed him onto the couch. It was the only piece of furniture we'd chosen together. I disliked the oversized grey cushions, but it had turned into my favorite place to spend my evenings. The other chairs in the room never felt as cozy, no matter how much I tried to break them in.

"I found something I thought you might like," Mitch said. I heard shyness in his voice and felt a little wary. I didn't want another piece of jewelry he expected me to wear to a company party. I sipped wine as he fished in his pockets, finally pulling out a folded piece of paper.

Smoothing it onto the wooden tray I arranged on one of the oversized cushions, I saw he'd torn the ad out of one of the weekly magazines that always littered the lobby and the sitting areas of his building. Slightly confused, I pushed up my lips in a smile. "I'll pass it along to Caroline," I said.

He looked as confused as I felt. "No, I thought you might want to go. I meant for it to be for you. Not that you couldn't invite Caro, if you wanted."

The ad for an antique auction a few hours outside of the city was something I'd have torn out myself, or bookmarked on the computer, before I left Raindrops on Roses. For a year or so after, I attempted to keep up with the treasure hunting I'd been so good at, but with picky eaters and a husband who got busier and busier with each turn of the moon, and eventually with Logan unexpectedly joining our family, I stopped noticing auctions or design trends or even the Pantone Color of the Year.

"I don't know when I'll find the time," I said, reaching across Mitchell and pulling my paper planner from the other side of the couch. Frustration mingled with tenderness for what he'd tried to do, but so many of the blocks in my calendar were filled. An hour at the school here, picking up things for the house there, and my days dwindled into a collection of errands that didn't allow for much differentiation between our children's lives and my own. Even the relief from stepping down from the silent auction wouldn't manifest itself as extra time for a few months.

His hand covered the calendar, forcing my eyes up into his face. Concern creased the corners of his eyes.

"Hey. I've been thinking lately about how you seem even more distracted since we asked Amy to come help a little more. Let's figure out something that works for you."

Guilt about the possible source of my distraction bit at me, and I bit back by speaking harshly. "Scheduling a nanny just ends up being another task on the never ending to-do list of our lives."

His shoulders sagged a little, but he held my gaze. "Then what would help? Hiring her for more hours? Me working from home more often?"

I sighed, dueling emotions colliding. "I don't know. I don't have anything that's mine anymore."

I couldn't tell if his eyes were reflecting my own hurt or showing me his for the first time. "I never asked you to do that. I thought, when you stopped working with Caro, that you wanted to take all of that energy and bring it into our home."

"I did. I do," I said. "I just feel lonely. Invisible."

"Oh, Gen. You're probably the most visible person I know. You're always right in the middle of things," he said. "None of us would even know where we were supposed to be if it wasn't for you."

"That's not me, though. That's being a wife and a mom and a volunteer and someone who's just getting things done. All the time."

"Do you want to go back to work?"

I thought of Raindrops on Roses, sunlight streaming through the windows. Caroline and I used to take turns bringing in coffee, even before anything even resembling a profit started flowing through the vintage register Caro's husband had rigged into a credit card system with a tablet and a prayer. For an instant, I could feel the stickiness of refinishing wax and the headache that came from working with oil paint late into the night. Then I remembered how impossible it had been to juggle Oli's occupational therapy appointments with investor meetings. I remembered Caroline's exasperation, and the way she'd sigh in resignation when I missed another deadline.

"Daddy! I thought I heard you," Logan padded into the room again, and we looked at each other hopelessly, the loaded question hanging unanswered between us.

∾

"Caro, do you believe in fate?"

Caroline sighed. We'd had this conversation before, impassioned and wrought with bias and hope, her belief system traipsing down paths mine would only wander so far before turning back to staunch practicality.

"I don't think I can have this conversation with you about Will," Caroline said. "I love you, but you don't get to pawn this situation off on a greater power."

"I was just asking your opinion," I said, tracing my finger around the top of the wine glass, something I always did when I felt nervousness twisting in my gut. My kids were cozy in bed and had been for the last hour. Our husbands were enjoying a rare night out: baseball and beer. I considered asking Mitchell if he'd trade nights, hosting Luke at our house while Caroline and I got dressed up and ate overpriced appetizers, but there had been something comforting about having her here. The wine was cheaper, and I was able to put on my fuzziest, warmest socks over my favorite leggings.

"You were asking for my permission," Caroline countered, and I wished I'd never brought it up.

"I just think it's got to mean *something* that I ran into him, of all people, when I feel so unsettled about everything," I said.

"But did you?" Caroline asked, pouring both of us a little more wine and gesturing to the couches in the other room. "Feel unsettled, I mean."

"I think so. I mean, yes. I just don't know if I recognized it as that," I said. I hated explaining myself to her. There had been a time where we'd been able to practically read each other's minds, when our lives had been barreling down such similar paths that it seemed sometimes like our thoughts were just as in sync as our dream for our own little store.

"I guess that doesn't even make sense," I said. "You probably don't feel like that very often, huh?"

"Luke and I are adopting a baby," Caroline blurted out, and I saw redness creep up her chest. Her fair skin always betrayed her emotions. "Maybe a toddler. We won't know until we know."

I almost dropped my wine. I knew they had struggled to get pregnant years before, testing and trying and going to more doctors' appointments than I could keep track of when I'd been drowning in diapers and midnight feedings for two

—and then three—infants. Soon after Logan had been born, Caroline had matter-of-factly told me they were done; they couldn't fathom going through any more testing or medical interventions. She talked vaguely about adoption as a future, abstract option, but she never really mentioned it again. As the store grew, more and more like Caroline's own child, I assumed an actual child had faded from their plans. I'd assumed incorrectly, obviously.

"Oh, honey! Congratulations," I collapsed on her in a hug, and soon we were both crying and laughing, and Will seemed as far away as he'd been for the past fifteen years.

"So yes, I get the unsettled feeling," Caroline laughed. "So much. Sometimes I think we're crazy for doing this and other times I don't believe we didn't do it sooner."

"I need to ask you about fate again," I said, thoughts clicking into place more quickly than they should have after a glass and a half of wine, mostly on an empty stomach, since we left the cheese tray in the kitchen.

"What? Why?" Caroline said, "You're supposed to be asking me if I've thought about whether we'll change her name or buy her those crazy hair bows you always see on babies. You're supposed to ask if I want you to come to China with us and hold our hands."

"No, listen. Seriously. You know what Mitchell and I were talking about last night? Literally not even twenty-four hours ago?"

"Probably not whether or not you should see Will again," Caroline mumbled.

"No," I said, unable to even get irritated with her comment after hearing her news. "We were talking about me going back to work. And now you drop this bombshell that you're adopting a baby, and you're going to be traveling to China more than once, and then you're going to have this little person depending on you, and I am thinking maybe there is fate out there, working in some weird way I can't even start to explain."

"You know I have people who help me in the store, right?" Caroline said, voice a little protective, and I couldn't blame her for that, not after how easily I walked away the first time.

"You have wonderful college students who take fabulous care of the store and have no idea how to do any of the millions of little things that make Raindrops on Roses special."

Caroline sighed. "You might be right. I was just talking to Luke about what in the world we would do about refinishing furniture, and what a nightmare it could be to go on buying excursions with a baby. Or a toddler. Shit, Gen. I'm going to have a child."

"A lucky child," I said. "And my kids are going to be so excited to have a cousin. Especially Char. She asks for a sister all the time, and we all know that ship isn't taking off from the dock again."

"Now that the news is out, I need to make something clear. Luke and I are not going to be moving in next door. I want to raise her in the city."

"I get it," I said, even though I would have said she was crazy just a few weeks ago. "There's so much to do there."

I hoped she didn't read anything into the comment; I hadn't yet told her about the folded postcard for the art exhibit Will had invited me to see.

∼

Mitchell stumbled into our room well past the hour of civil conversation, but I flipped onto my side to chat with him anyway. I couldn't remember the last time he let himself drink too many beers with a friend, and I wondered how we'd let ourselves get so wrapped up in life that we allowed the living part to slip aside.

"Did Luke tell you?" I asked, my words bubbling out after dancing around in my head for hours after Caroline had gone home.

"I don't know," he said, laughing. "I don't believe I stayed out this late when I'm leaving in the morning."

"They're going to have a baby. They're adopting a baby." I steered him back to the conversation I wanted to have, ignoring yet another conversation about his work travel plans.

A goofy smile took over his entire face. I estimated half came from happiness and half from hops, but I still loved watching it reach all the way to his eyes.

"You're going to be such a fantastic aunt, Gen," he said.

I agreed, but it still stung just a little to hear my role once again relegated to caretaker status. I smiled and let my other thought fly.

"I told Caro I'd go back to Raindrops. She's going to need so much more help than she even knows, you know?"

The smile remained on his face, but I saw, or maybe imagined, a slight shadow slide across his eyes.

"And she was OK with that? Even after everything that happened?" he asked.

"Yes. I think, at least. We talked about it for a long time," I said. Caroline and I had even gotten to the point of pulling up the store's orders and inventory, looking at places where I could help immediately.

"So you made a decision," he said.

Gooseflesh rose on my arms, prickling into the air.

"I did. We talked about this, remember? You told me we needed to figure out something that worked for me."

He nodded. "I know. I just...we never finished talking about it, you know?"

"I know," I said. Guilt and irritation mingled with the remnants of wine, and my news suddenly tasted sour on my tongue instead of exciting. Resentment flared.

"It's a big decision for the whole family," he said. "I thought we'd make that sort of decision together."

"God, Mitchell. I thought you'd understand. It's not full time. I don't plan on just abandoning our family to its own devices."

"Don't, Gen. I don't want to fight about it," he said, reaching for me.

"I didn't think we were fighting. I thought I was sharing something with you."

"I'm just surprised you decided without saying anything to me."

"It just kind of happened," I said, sighing. "Sometimes things fall into place in ways you don't expect. Don't you think it's important to grab those opportunities?"

He inhaled, and I could see him gathering his thoughts, searching for something that would make sense to him. Finally, the smile on his face reached his eyes again.

"What the hell, Gen. Why not? You've always managed to pull everything together before. Why would this be any different?"

Even though I had never thought of myself in quite that way, I basked in his confidence. It was one of the things I loved most about him almost immediately: his implicit trust that I could do the things that seemed out of reach. I touched my forehead to his and trailed my fingers up his arm, but he was practically snoring by the time I reached his shoulder.

He left in the morning before the sun rose, with a lingering kiss that uncomfortably conjured thoughts of Will. I wavered about the decision for two days, picking up my phone to cancel probably twenty times, but as Mitch left our bedroom, I knew I'd attend the opening. I needed to finish whatever it was that had managed to worm its way even into my dreams.

The kids were thrilled to welcome Amy into the house for the night, and I promised her I wouldn't be too late, just like I promised Charlotte I'd take her to an art installation soon. The juxtaposition of making plans with my daughter that mirrored plans with Will unnerved me just as much as how carefully I'd chosen what to wear. I wanted to hustle Charlotte out of my closet as she ran fingers over my clothes, telling me why I should and shouldn't wear certain pieces. Everything about tonight felt heavy and wrought with meaning, and I forced myself to weigh that guilt against the gulf of uncertainty in my heart.

Spring felt different on Will's stoop than it did in areas of the city with which I was more familiar. Raindrops on Roses was surrounded by little stores and enough essential oils to drive out the lingering scent of garbage I remembered from my college days, but his block teemed with traffic and food trucks, the green space of nearby Central Park a concept rather than a promise of fresh air. I hesitated at the buzzer. We agreed to meet at his place, confirmed by text and anticipation, but I hadn't considered how it might feel to be buzzed up to his apartment. I considered scurrying down the street for a coffee, texting to ask if he wanted anything, asking him to meet me there instead.

I flexed my fingers, staring at my wedding ring and reminding myself I hadn't done anything wrong. A broken bouquet of roses lay abandoned near a parking meter, the detached petals an ominous warning about expectations. Feeling guilty over the possibility of impropriety made it seem like I'd already made a choice about how things might go with him. I jammed my finger into the small button, daring myself to face the decision head on.

He made it for me, answering, "Be right down," in a rushed voice that made me feel even more foolish. All the talk between Caroline and me had made it seem like Will's motivation had to be nefarious, when it was still plausible he was just looking for a friend in a city that hadn't left him with many.

He pushed the door open with a smile. No matter what else I might have imagined about the evening, the sweeping glance and consequent admiration felt tangible, like a warm breeze pressing against my skin. He shook a cigarette into my hand without hesitation. The familiar rhythm felt like a betrayal of my marriage more than his eyes on my body. We walked in silence for a few minutes. I remembered how this had once felt with Mitchell, before we had to cram our time together with conversations about the kids' schedules or school obligations, before our time together felt like one more thing to schedule.

"I'm going back to Raindrops on Roses," I blurted, when the silence became something palpable that had to be broken.

"Really?" His raised eyebrow felt like a secret between us. "So you'll be in the city more often?"

I hadn't considered that he might see the decision as something to do with him. His supposition changed something, and the familiarity that had seemed intimate felt cloying. I'd made a decision that seemed almost selfish, that hadn't taken anyone's feelings into consideration as much as my own, and it felt like he wanted a part of that. I dropped my cigarette into a potted plant, knowing it was still littering but feeling like it was a little better than dropping it directly on the sidewalk to be ground into flatness by the thousands of feet that wouldn't even notice it was there.

"Well, yes, of course. I can't work at Raindrops on Roses

without coming into the city." I didn't try to hide the annoyance in my voice. "But the decision didn't hinge on how often I'd be here," I said. My hands emphasized my words, sweeping in an arc at the teeming sidewalk, making sure it included him, unsure why I still felt desire mingled with my anger.

"I didn't mean anything by that," he said, laughing, though neither of us believed it.

"I doubt that. You always mean something," I said, trying to hurt him, though I could tell by his eyes that I hadn't come close to a blow.

"I thought you wanted to be here, to see something new," he said. He stopped, his knowledge of our location an advantage when it came to ending a conversation that felt rife with innuendo.

Black and white photographs lined the walls, well lit, though the middle of the gallery was dim with murmured conversation and cheap wine in plastic cups. I'd forgotten the energy of an opening night, the frantic anticipation of how the installation would be received. I closed my eyes, letting myself forget who I was with, letting the mood wash over me with the promise of seduction. The photographs could have been of anything; I simply wanted to be surrounded by tangible creativity.

When Will's hand pressed gently into my lower back, I accepted the touch and let him guide me to the makeshift bar. I'd forgotten this, too, the raw beauty on display in a city teeming with broke models and aspiring actors who worked private parties for extra cash. I tucked my clutch under my arm and asked for a glass of the Pinot Grigio, though I imagined it would be a little too sweet for my liking. It was. I drank it anyway, steady sips that ignored the taste and delivered alcohol that quieted my racing thoughts enough to wander between photos without worrying whether or not

Will was walking with me. He was, letting my interest and pace guide our steps. A second glass of wine seemed like a terrible idea but I accepted it from him without a word, eventually following him out to the street where we leaned against the wall to smoke.

I let my head drop back, the bricks snagging my hair. One of my favorite things about Manhattan had always been the columns of light snaking into the sky via windows towering above my head. Years ago, when I couldn't sleep, I'd walk up and down the sidewalk, eventually staring up at the skyscrapers and finding comfort knowing so many other people were chasing their thoughts into the sky as well. Stars punctuated the night outside my house now. Oliver obsessively described the constellations, but I could never find comfort in their order, and I never went outside to stare at them when I couldn't sleep.

"This feels right," I said. I could feel how close he was, and I didn't care.

"I know," he said. His tone was even, noncommittal.

"I didn't even know how much I missed it," I said. I meant the city, the energy, the freedom from having to answer forty-seven questions each time a minute of silence punctuated our lives. I knew Will couldn't understand. I think I even knew how he would take my statement, and I made it anyway.

My cigarette smoldered between my fingers when he kissed me. I think I dropped it, letting it burn into a stub on the ground. His body pressed mine against the brick, an unending line of contact from our lips to where our legs scissored between each other. For an eternity, I let it happen, and then I kissed him back, tongues tangling in a slow, torturous dance we'd tried a lifetime ago. Every nerve ending in my body reached out to him, and I wasn't sure I had any breath in my lungs when I gently shifted away from his mouth. I didn't move away from his body, though, needing to capture every moment.

"I'm in love with Mitchell," I said. My choice of words was deliberate. Simply reminding him of my marriage wouldn't be enough; I knew that. It hadn't been enough for either of us as we inched toward this moment.

"Can you tell me you feel like this," he whispered, closing the distance between our mouths with another searing kiss, "when you're with him?"

Never, I thought, and I knew it was true. Nothing between Mitchell and I had ever pulsed with the savage pleasure I felt with Will. I needed to feel it one more time, to know I could have it in my life if only I wanted to let everything else—including myself—fall apart.

"I can," I said. He saw the lie in my eyes and didn't move away from my body.

"I am in awe of you," Will said. His throaty words shot through my veins, closing my eyes and making me want to forget everything else in the world. Instead I pushed against his chest, breaking contact and finding my breath.

"Maybe you are," I said, pushing back my hair back from my temples. "But that's not how you felt all those years ago. Mitchell loved me, Mitchell was in awe of me before I even knew what I could become."

Seconds ticked into over a minute, and I thought this would feel better than an anvil on my chest. I wanted to walk away, but I accepted one of the last two cigarettes in his pack and sank to one of the cement planters lining the street. I smoked so I wouldn't kiss him again, so I wouldn't take back my decision, so I wouldn't ask him to stay. He might have known those things, and he might not have. Just like fifteen years ago, his eyes had shuttered against me, and the wryness in his smile felt like a judgment instead of a secret.

"You don't get to be in awe of me now," I said. I wanted,

for the first time in years, to feel that way about myself. To weave together the parts of my life that had frayed. I pictured showing Charlotte how to tell the difference between real wood and veneer, pictured her watching me wear safety glasses instead of another little black dress.

"Let me walk you back to the subway," he said.

I knew before the words left his lips that I would refuse whatever he offered. If I didn't, I wouldn't be able to say no to anything else he offered, ever again. For an instant, his facade fell apart, and I could see anguish in his eyes. I hoped, selfishly, that he could see mine, too, that he could see how close I'd come to falling apart in his arms. I stood, pressing my hand gently into his shoulder so he wouldn't.

"I can find my way," I said.

"I know," he said.

In a final moment of weakness, I cradled his face in my hands, brushed his lips with my thumb, let him rest his forehead against my sternum. Before he could hear my quickening heart, I stepped back and turned away, walking toward the life I had finally, consciously, chosen.

∼

ALSO BY ANGELA AMMAN

Collected Short Fiction
Nothing Goes Away

Anthology features
Metaphysical Gravity
Echoes in Darkness

Christmas Anthology Features
Joy
Merry Little Christmas
Secret Santas
Atlantic to Pacific

EXCERPT FROM NOTHING GOES AWAY

SPLINTERS

Staying in Ann Arbor for the summer was a novelty for him and a necessity for me. Our pasts and futures were hazy flashes we didn't visit, choosing instead to live in a balloon of today that we populated with debates on music and the sustainability of nuclear power. We'd visited various friends all summer, floating in the Great Lakes and taking turns driving his father's spare SUV back and forth so we could delve into Organic Chem after a weekend of poorly mixed Bloody Marys and cheap tequila shooters. This weekend was a sprawling beach house somewhere between Ann Arbor and Chicago, the combination of college kids and old high school friends confusing us all.

I'd shed my light sweater as we walked to this picnic table. The cotton trailed from my fingers the way I trailed just a step behind Luke, unsure if we were really walking to the same place. My wrists ached from leaning back on the splinted picnic bench, but shifting my weight would tilt the balance of our conversation. A cigarette smoldered between my fingers, though I hadn't smoked in months. After settling into my dorm room, I'd ground out my past like bits of ash; the shadow of what remained faded a little each day. I ignored the way the slim cylinder felt natural between my fingers; some habits, once broken, should stay broken.

"Do you ever think about going back?" his voice floated the few inches to my ear.

"To the moon?" I asked, trying to focus on the heavy silver orb and not the sticky heat connecting us, our arms touching from elbow to wrist. Blinking hadn't done anything to clear the blurriness of the stars. I reveled in it, floating somewhere between who I had been a year ago, who I was, and who I could be with him.

Luke rocked forward from our semi-reclined position, and I followed. I needed to stay in his orbit. My lips hungrily sought the cigarette, wanting to inhale a part of him. I couldn't breathe from the spiked lemonade and the pungent smoke and when his eyes found mine I was reminded he was as close to sober as I was to drunk.

"Do you ever think about going back to Oklahoma?"

∽

EXCERPT FROM METAPHYSICAL GRAVITY

IN HIS HANDS

"Darling, he made a mistake. Lord knows your Daddy's made a couple in his day," she said.

My stomach turned slightly, and even all the Botox in St. Tammany Parish wouldn't have kept my eyebrows from hitting my hairline. Realizing how her words had sounded, my mother blushed furiously.

"Oh! That is not what I meant, Lainey. I just meant we've made it through some rough patches."

Blushing suited her, especially against her pale gray silk. If I didn't say something quickly I was going to have to bury my face in her shoulder. She could never know I wanted nothing more than to slide my gorgeous, glittering diamond back on my finger. But I knew he'd never stop cheating, just like I'd known it when I found a sparkly tube of lip gloss in an awful coral shade wedged between his twin bed and the wall in his cramped law school apartment. Our friends smoothed it over back then, my brothers making excuses for him and my girlfriends reassuring me I was much cuter, funnier and more wonderful than she could possibly be.

Gently perching next to me on the bed, Mama's gentle hand carefully smoothed my hair and rested against my cheek. I saw the worry in her eyes, softer and warmer than her voice ever was, and my resolve wavered a little more. I'd inherited more than her pale hair and inability to turn any color but lobster red in the sun; my words burned hotter than my anger, and forgiveness lingered at the surface of my fury over Cody's latest betrayal.

"I've always loved that photo," Mama said, fingers sliding over the charmingly tarnished silver frame on the nightstand. Cody, my Grammy and I were posed in front of a Cyprus tree outside of the high school, my royal blue graduation gown somehow managing to look much cooler in the photograph than I remember it feeling that day. You could see the humidity in the hair beginning to curl around my temples, but my eyes fell to my grandmother's right hand. Hanging carefully at her side, her fingers were wrapped in a pair of her delicate gloves. Around my seventeenth birthday she'd taken to wearing them all the time, swollen joints hidden beneath kid leather, linen or sateen, every color of the rainbow placed carefully in the top drawer of her bureau.

∽

EXCERPT FROM JOY

AIRPORT CHRISTMAS

Margot gave silent thanks to TSA prescreening, just as she did every time she bypassed snaking lines--and got to keep on her beloved riding boots. She couldn't imagine not traveling with them, especially as she made her way back to the snowy northern city she called home, but schlepping them in her luggage annoyed her. Of course, this time, her luggage was being stowed in the belly of the plane, instead of awkwardly lofted into the overhead bins on the plane. Today, though, the lines were about equal--though she still got to keep on her shoes.

People stared at the monitors worriedly. Margot tried not to worry too much about Bert's weather warning. Her flight to Buffalo was still scheduled and listed as on-time, though she noted an alarming number of incoming flights seemed to be canceling at rapid rates, especially those with departing cities in the northeast.

She pulled her phone from her bag, the instinct to message Vance as natural as breathing. They'd spent the past few years cobbling together their own private form of communication: texts, voice messages, and video calls all wove together to help them feel connected when they were generally traveling in opposite directions. Even now, with anger and hurt coursing through her body with each heartbeat, she couldn't disentangle herself from the knowledge that he was in Los Angeles or the automatic calculating of time zones. She replaced the phone carefully, no longer sure how to speak to the man she loved.

"Where you headed, hon?" The question shook her out of her own thoughts.

The couple staring at the oversized screen were obviously not flying to Buffalo. Tropical flowers practically jumped off his shirt, and flamingos strutted across her neat shift dress. Margot idly wondered if she and Vance would spend retirement in coordinating clothes, before cooly realizing she'd recently stashed papers into her suitcase that meant she and Vance weren't likely to ever worry about coordinating clothes again. Her mumbled answer to the polite query felt rude, but so did subjecting the unsuspecting couple to the tears threatening to fall.

Coffee would help. Coffee always helped. Even with smaller than normal crowds, the line at the coffee shop twisted outside of the kiosk. With her phone in her bag, she quickly felt its absence in her palm. She crossed and uncrossed her arms, unsure what exactly to do without scrolling through social media or email.

"Going north?" The unexpected question caused her to stumble over her own answer. She would have thought years of travel and visiting countless new offices would have made her a little better at striking up random conversations.

"Yes, Buffalo," she finally said.

"No, really? Me, too," the question-asker said.

He reminded her of Vance immediately. She sighed. With her husband swirling around in her head, of course any man with slightly shaggy blond hair and an easy smile would remind her of Vance. This stranger didn't really look much like Vance at all, with a bit of a beard and a battered fleece that looked like it actually saw its way around a hiking trail.

"Are you worried about the weather?" Margot asked. She wanted him to keep smiling at her, and the only way to do that was to keep talking.

"Nah," he said. "We're used to that, right?"

"Well, sure. But we're not the ones flying the plane," Margot said.

He grinned. "Not today, at least." His eyes trailed over the top of her head, and she realized she might have just lost his attention. "Your turn, I think."

Cheeks burning for thinking he might be flirting, just a little, she hurriedly ordered the biggest coffee she could and retreated to the nearby bathroom. A quick glance in the bathroom mirror reminded her of one of her grandmother's favorite pieces of advice. She dug in her bag and took an extra minute to dig the tube of red lipstick from the bottom of her favorite makeup. Nothing seemed impossible while wearing red lipstick.

∽

ABOUT ANGELA AMMAN

Angela's writing explores how women interact with the world around them. She holds a BA in English from Michigan State University and an MA in Education from Wayne State University, and previously taught 6th grade Language Arts and 8th grade mathematics. For four years, she co-directed Listen to Your Mother Metro Detroit, bringing stories to the stage to celebrate the courage and connectivity of live storytelling. She is the managing editor at Savvy Sassy Moms, a writer for Take Flight Social Media Consulting, and was an editor for Write on Edge, where she co-curated three volumes of PRECIPICE: THE LITERARY ANTHOLOGY OF WRITE ON EDGE. Her short stories and essays have been featured in her debut collection, NOTHING GOES AWAY, and anthologies like METAPHYSICAL GRAVITY and MY OTHER EX: WOMEN'S TRUE STORIES ABOUT LOSING AND LEAVING FRIENDS.

She spends part of every day trying to convince her husband to buy into her color-coded family calendar system and another part of it figuring out where she put down her coffee mug. When her attention falters, she shares flash fiction, lightning quick book reviews, and personal vignettes on her website. She lives in Metro Detroit with her husband and two children. When she should be sleeping, she's adding more books to her library hold queue and contemplating whether the perfect mascara exists.

www.angelaamman.com

- facebook.com/AngelaAmmanWrites
- twitter.com/angelaamman
- instagram.com/angelaamman

ABOUT THE PUBLISHER

Bannerwing Books is a co-op of independent authors, founded in Massachusetts in 2012 and currently residing in the ether between Boston, Detroit, and Paso Robles.

www.bannerwingbooks.com

facebook.com/bannerwingbooks
twitter.com/bannerwingbooks

Made in the USA
Monee, IL
04 November 2019